FIVE O'CLOCK TWIST

FIVE O'CLOCK TWIST

AN INSPECTOR REBECCA MAYFIELD MYSTERY

JOANNE PENCE

QUAIL HILL PUBLISHING

Quail Hill Publishing

PO Box 64

Eagle, ID 83616

Visit our website at www.quailhillpublishing.net

First Quail Hill Publishing E-book: January 2017

First Quail Hill Print Book: January 2017

Second Quail Hill Print Book: August 2018

FIVE O'CLOCK TWIST

1

It was midnight, and San Francisco Homicide Inspector Rebecca Mayfield stood alone on a cold, desolate beach. The biting wind off the Pacific Ocean hit hard. Earlier the fog had rolled in, heavy, thick, and wet. She hugged her black leather jacket tight against her body.

Rebecca and her partner, Bill Sutter, were the current "on-call" team which meant they were the first detectives sent to any suspicious death in the city. Tonight's call from the police dispatcher directed Rebecca to Baker's Beach.

The beach was nearly a mile long, edging what had once been a U.S. Army base, the Presidio of San Francisco. It was now part of the Golden Gate National Recreation Area. She had driven onto its parking lot which was the only area where the street was level with the beach. Past it, the street rose quickly following cliffs that skirted the beach all the way to the Golden Gate Bridge.

The lot's street lamps, blanketed by fog, cast an eerie glow over the deserted surroundings. No squad cars with uniformed police secured the scene. Also absent were the medical examiner's team, the crime scene unit, a photographer, and all the myriad others who always showed up at potential homicides. All was quiet except for the sound of waves against the shore, and the strong, persistent wind.

She couldn't even hear traffic noise, which was particularly unnerving for a city cop.

Rebecca was sure she had been sent to the wrong place. Although she was often the first detective to arrive, the uniforms were always there. This was crazy.

She took out her phone and was about to call the dispatcher when she saw a flashlight. "You from Homicide?" a male voice called. She looked, but could barely make out the figure holding the large bright light directed at her.

"Mayfield." Rebecca identified herself and held up her badge. "You are?" she asked, trying to shield her eyes from the bright light to see at least an outline of the person she was speaking to.

"Officer Garcia. Crime scene's at the far end of the beach. Just walk north. You'll find it."

"Where is everyone?" she asked.

Garcia took a few steps backwards. "The officers are parked at the top of the cliff. There's a pathway down, a shortcut, so they took it. But the fog is even thicker now, so it might be making the rocks we took kind of wet and slick. It's a longer walk to take the beach, but probably safer. They sent me here to tell you and the others the best way to find them. Sorry that you got here before I did. Must have confused you a bit. Anyway, we're all on the same page now. I'm heading out to the entrance to the parking lot. I'll wave the CSI and others in here."

This was just plain weird, Rebecca thought. The beam from the officer's flashlight continued to blind her. She turned her head away from him. "Okay. Guess I walk," she said.

"You can't miss it," the officer called. He was already some distance away, heading towards the street. "Just before the rocks."

Almost the entire beach lay "just before the rocks." No wonder the uniforms had taken a shortcut. Her boots sank into the sand with each step, making the going slow. She had been out here a couple of times at a beach party, times when the evening was warm, when moonlight cast a glow over the water, and stars filled the night sky in a sparkling array. But tonight was different. No light made its way through the fog, and even the lighthouse out on the Farallon Islands might have been extinguished.

The briny smell of the sea was so thick it seemed to attach itself to her skin, hair, and even her lips.

She flicked on her small pocket flashlight. Droplets of fog turned everything in the light's path into a shimmering halo. She had to direct the beam downward simply to see where she was stepping. Something about all this felt "off." She paused. Maybe she should wait for the others and walk out there together with them.

But Officer Garcia had most likely radioed the other uniforms that she was on her way. They would be looking for her. Was she supposed to say she was too "scared" to walk on a beach alone, given her training and the powerful weapon she carried? No way. She'd never live it down. She squared her shoulders and trudged on, her jeans-clad legs taking long, purposeful strides.

While the southern beach area, near the parking lot, was popular on warm, sunny days, especially since nude bathing—typically "San Francisco"—was allowed, the northern portion was a different story. The sandy beach ended at a low-lying wall of rocky outcrops. Climbing over the boulders led to several small, secluded cove-like areas butting up against steep cliffs, and separated one from the other by massive, slippery rocks.

She couldn't help but chuckle to herself as she thought of how her partner, Bill Sutter, was going to react when he was told to walk down a dark, freezing beach at midnight to find the crime scene. He'd swear a blue streak over getting sand in his shoes, and that was just the start of it.

He hated anything that caused him to feel less than absolutely in charge. Sometimes he was fine, but other times, he acted as if he was afraid of his own shadow, let alone the dark. He was often referred to as "Never-Take-a-Chance Bill" because of it.

Richie Amalfi, the man she was currently dating, swore that if she wasn't careful, Sutter was going to get her killed. Richie said she needed a partner who had her back, not one who'd cut and run first chance he got. She thought he was wrong about that, and perhaps, wrong about a lot of things. Including their relationship.

She had given Richie a lot of thought lately; too much thought, in fact. It made her heart heavy to think about him, and all that would never be between them. But she was nothing if not practical, and the practical side of her nature told her it was time to move on.

Yet, trying to put him out of her mind was difficult, if not impossible. In fact, he had phoned her a couple of times as she drove out here tonight. They were working on a case together. Not that she should have been involving him in her homicide investigations, but as usual, he seemed to know the people who had gotten caught up in a murder, and she found his knowledge of them helpful.

She didn't answer his calls. Given the time of night and all that had happened earlier between them, his calls couldn't be anything but personal. For the moment, she needed to concentrate on where she was going and her reason for going there. Not on Richie.

As she continued along the beach, the hill that edged it grew higher and steeper, resulting in a cliff-like edifice that trapped the fog and made it increasingly thick. Now, swirling billows of mist hugged the ground, and the aura of light her flashlight created was so blinding she could scarcely see beyond her hand.

There had been a time when Rebecca enjoyed the heavy San Francisco fog. "Pea soup," the old timers called it. But that was years ago when she first came to the city, and before she had seen an eternity of ugliness on her job that muted the city's charm.

As she continued towards the rocks, the silence bothered her. She should be hearing something from the secured crime scene by now. Instead, the only sounds she heard were the lapping of ocean waves against the shore and the occasional, mournful call of a foghorn.

Up ahead, she could just make out the rocks.

And no crime scene.

The unwanted thought struck that there was never a crime scene out here.

Her breathing quickened, and the skin on her arms prickled.

How could that be? The police dispatcher ...

The dull worry that something was dreadfully wrong turned into a thunderous roar. Every fiber of her being told her to run. She dropped the lit flashlight to the ground, escaping into the fog. Then, instead of heading back down the beach in the direction she came from, she ran as fast as she could in the loose sand towards the cliffs.

As she did, a hail of gunshots went off directed at the light. She heard the sound of metal and glass exploding as her flashlight went out.

She forced herself to keep going as shots flew all around. She hurtled towards the cliffs; only there might she find some kind of shelter. The rapid-fire roar of the fusillade told her that her adversary was using a semi-automatic rifle, a serious killing machine. The shooter was firing blind—even a night scope was useless in the dense mist.

She didn't shoot back, thankful for the shielding fog, and knowing her chance of hitting a shooter she couldn't see was nil.

When she reached the cliff, she all but hugged it, trying to find some boulder, some crevice, anything that might provide shelter. A shot pinged near her and she saw a flash. The shooter must have realized she was searching the cliffs for shelter rather than trying to return to the parking lot.

Finally, she located a spot where a bit of the cliff face curved inward, eroded by the constant pummeling of wind and surf. She hugged the inlet, her back against it, standing as straight and flat as possible. Another hail of bullets, one after the other, cut a swath across the cliff face where she had been standing just seconds earlier. When the shooting stopped, she returned fire, again and again, aiming in the direction of the flash from the firearm.

There were no other cops around, and now she knew there wouldn't be. She'd been set up and directed out here to get her alone. To kill her.

She was scared, more scared than she'd ever been. She didn't want to die.

More shots came her way, and she fired back again and again, even though she recognized that, just that as she had done earlier, her attacker kept moving. She made a mental count of how many bullets she had used, and how few she had left. She knew the way this was going, all the attacker had to do was to wait until she was out of ammunition.

She lay flat on the ground. With both hands on her SIG Sauer, her arms outstretched, she waited for the shooter to move closer. One on one. Whoever saw the other first, she believed, would be the one to live.

2

en days earlier...

Rebecca hurried across the narrow alley to the building that housed her tiny two-room apartment. It was dark, nearly nine at night, but the night was pleasant, and a full moon shone brightly. She was glad to be home, glad she had no complex homicide filling her days and tormenting her dreams at night.

The few street lamps cast a soft, golden glow on Mulford Alley, but as she took out her house keys, an uneasy feeling crept over her. She had never been one to pay any attention to "feelings" or "intuition," but lately, she had met people, and one person in particular, who suggested she needed to listen to what her instincts were telling her, and not only to her too-logical brain. She listened now. Before she unlocked the door by the side of the garage, she made it a point to scan the area all around her.

And, just as her logical self had told her, no one was there.

She softly chuckled as she put the key in the lock. Such nervousness was a common ailment for anyone who was a cop these days, and especially for one whose job centered on murders. She opened the door to a tunnel-like breezeway, then walked through it to the backyard. Her "garden apartment," aka a glorified storeroom, faced the yard.

Usually, once past the dark breezeway and near her front door, she began to relax. But for some reason, the jangly sense that struck her outside still hadn't let up.

Maybe because it was Saturday night, she told herself. Usually, that meant she would be seeing Richie Amalfi. But tonight she wouldn't and, despite the fact it was her own doing, it bothered her.

Next, she unlocked her apartment door. Needing to pass through two locked doors before reaching the inside of her residence made this the perfect set-up for a somewhat paranoid cop living alone. Also, this arrangement caused her to have the yard pretty much to herself, which she considered to be the best part of her living space.

Inside the apartment, she greeted her little dog, Spike, and then changed into comfortable clothes. With a fresh cup of coffee in hand, she and Spike went into the backyard with his favorite red ball. "Spike" was an ironic name for a tiny Chihuahua-Chinese Crested Hairless mix, but it was his when she decided to keep him after finding him at a crime scene. No one else wanted him, not even to adopt him from the Humane Society. Even she had to admit that his pinkish skin with large brown spots, and hairless body except for white tufts of hair on his head, feet, and tail were pretty peculiar looking. Some people were cruel enough to say he was ugly, and to say it right out loud where he could hear them. She understood completely why he tried to bite loud-mouthed strangers.

The bottom line was that Rebecca adored him. And now, she couldn't help but smile at his joy and exuberance running after the ball.

She was glad someone was filled with joy. She wasn't.

And she was sure it was all because of Richie.

The problem was a simple one. A short time back, he'd gotten himself into a situation where she feared he had been killed. The way she felt had focused her on all he had come to mean to her, how important he was, how much she cared—or more—about him. And it worried her.

The more time she spent with him, the more attached to him she was becoming. He was fun, exciting even. And surprisingly thoughtful and caring towards her, not to mention generous ... and sexy. And good-looking. And sweet to Spike.

Even her sister liked him, which should have been the kiss of death.

Damn.

But she also knew that their relationship would go nowhere. Richie had made it clear he worried about her being a cop, about the dangers of the job, and she didn't see them moving forward as a couple as long as she continued with it. And she wasn't about to give up a job that she loved and felt was important.

Ironically, despite everything, she also recognized that as much as their relationship was bad for her, it might be even worse for him. He was surrounded by women in his work, and she was sure there were plenty that would make a lot better wife for him than she ever could. And the guy needed to settle down. The more she got to know him, and to care about him, the more obvious that became. His fiancée had been killed some years ago, and he was finally getting over the loss. But the danger she was often in and his resulting fear of losing her was like constantly tearing the scab off a wound where his emotions were concerned.

She could tell that he wanted someone to fill the void in his life. But she didn't think she was that person. She liked being the one to bring bad guys to justice. Was that so wrong of her? And so, the time had come to stop seeing him. To break it off. End it ... whatever "it" was. Goodbye. So long. *Finito*.

Her choice was Richie versus everything else she valued about her life, and she felt it was better to cut it off now, before things got any more serious between them, before she'd have to admit she was in love with him, and while she could still walk away. Or not.

Sometimes she really made herself sick.

She was dismally contemplating life without Richie when Spike suddenly stopped chasing the ball and looked up at the flat where Kiki Nuñez lived. He began to growl.

The building that housed Rebecca's ground-floor apartment also had two upper stories. Kiki lived right above Rebecca, and the top floor comprised the home of their landlord, Bradley Frick.

Rebecca looked up to see what had caught Spike's attention. Kiki's lights were on, but Rebecca couldn't see any reason for Spike's growling.

Kiki was in her late forties, divorced with two grown children, and she owned an upscale spa that did extremely well. She had a big heart, an over-sized, vivacious personality, and a casual flirtatiousness that caused her to collect men with ease. Rebecca wished she had half of Kiki's ability along those lines.

Before Richie entered Rebecca's life, she spent a lot of time with Kiki. Often, on nights like this one, Kiki would come out to join her, her high-heeled mules clattering loudly on the back stairs, with a bottle of chilled white wine in one hand and two glasses in the other. The women would sit and enjoy the wine as they talked of life, love, interesting men they'd met, and what it all meant. And they would laugh. That was one thing Rebecca loved about Kiki. Coming from a job so filled with death and sadness, she found it wonderful to be around someone who enjoyed life as thoroughly as her neighbor.

She realized she should talk to Kiki about the problem of Richie. Kiki was a clear-eyed rationalist, and she'd be able to help Rebecca figure out if she was being logical or crazy to break up with a man she enjoyed being with so very much.

Spike's growls grew louder.

Rebecca stood, trying to see what was upsetting her dog.

Spike suddenly began to bark. He rarely barked.

The feeling of being watched that Rebecca had had from the time she'd approached her building tonight returned again, tenfold. She moved towards the back stairs that led up to Kiki's flat. Spike grew more agitated, running to the stairs and back to her. Rebecca picked him up, put him in her apartment, grabbed her gun, and all but flew up the stairs to Kiki's back door.

Once there, she knocked hard and loud. When she received no answer, she knocked again and called Kiki's name as she peered into the window near the door that faced the kitchen. She was horrified to see the kitchen table away from the wall in a skewed position, and a chair on its side on the floor. Rebecca tried the doorknob. It turned.

She opened the door wide.

It made a high-pitched squeal, but other than that, there was no sound coming from the apartment. She crept forward.

From the kitchen, she entered the dining room, then the living room. Both appeared undisturbed. She turned towards the bedrooms and stopped.

Kiki lay in the hallway, a pool of blood around her head.

Richie Amalfi stood at the back of his nightclub, Big Caesar's. Located not far from San Francisco's famous Fisherman's Wharf area, it had been set up to look like the lush establishments of the 1930's and '40's with white linen-covered tables around a dance floor, a big band and singer, and an elaborate appetizer menu. Richie wore an elegant black suit and black bow tie to go along with the dressy ambiance of the place. Since he had a trim build, stood a little under six feet tall, with dark brown eyes and wavy black hair, purposefully worn just a tad long, the clothes on him looked James Bond suave rather than like some wedding party escapee.

Surrounding him was a group of customers including a couple of women who openly vied for Richie's attention despite their dates. The group was laughing and telling amusing tales. Or, mainly, it was Richie telling stories while the others listened with rapt attention.

The dance area was filled, as usual, when the big band began playing the old jazz and swing favorite, Cab Calloway's "Minnie the Moocher." Hearing it, Richie all but cringed, knowing what was coming. The music was fairly soft until the customers loudly joined in singing the "Hi dee hi dee hi dee hi" scat refrain. The raucous cacophony quickly started getting on Richie's nerves. It was all he could do not to pull the plug on the sound system and tell everybody to go the hell home. He maintained a smile as he escaped from the group by telling them how sorry he was that he had to 'mingle.' He was heading for his office when another group of customers stopped him, smiling with anticipation to talk to the popular club owner. At the same time, he noticed his two closest friends, Vito Grazioso and Henry Ian Tate, III, aka "Shay," enter the club. Vito and Shay helped him handle those difficult and specialized jobs that were the real source of Richie's income.

The customers introduced themselves, and by force of habit, Richie did all he could to commit each name to memory. He'd learned, over the years, that you never knew when such information would come in handy. "It's great to meet all of you," he said as they shook hands, smiling at each person as if he or she was the most important person in the world at that moment, and not giving any hint that he wanted to get away as quickly as possible. "I hope you're enjoying yourselves tonight."

"It's wonderful," they gushed.

"Thank you so much for coming," he said. "I truly appreciate it." He then excused himself and went off to meet Vito and Shay.

"What the hell took you so long?" He hurried with them back to his office.

Vito and Shay caught each other's eyes and didn't reply.

They entered the office, a large space, designed by Richie when he took over ownership of the club. On one side were a walnut desk, bookcases, and plush leather chair, and other side held a sofa, side chairs, and a mini bar. Blown-up photos of the great jazz and swing performers of the last century—people like Ella Fitzgerald, Billy Holiday, Louis Armstrong, Frank Sinatra, and Dean Martin—hung on the walls. The office also had a private bathroom with a shower. Richie had no idea why or if he'd ever need the shower, but since he'd put in the bathroom, why not?

They all sat in their usual seats, the sofa for Vito, and a side chair for each of the other two. Richie had a new job for them, a typical job, involving a guy who gambled too much at a floating poker game organized for the Bay Area's high-roller elites. Richie's client lost big, and now he was supposed to pay off—but had nothing to pay off with unless he sold either some property or some of his wife's jewelry. It was Richie's job to make a deal with the organizers to keep the man's marriage, if not his finances, intact. And from the whole mess to squeeze out enough of a payment for himself, Shay and Vito, that it was worth their time and effort to get involved.

"So, you got all this straight, Vito?" Richie gritted his teeth as he waited for his friend's answer. "Or do I have to go over it again?"

"I got it, boss. Wha'dya think? You know you can count on me with these things." Vito tried not to show that his feelings were hurt, but they clearly were. He was a bear of a man, although a not-too-tall bear, with a barrel-shaped body covered in a perpetually worn tan car coat whose pockets bulged with food and mysteries unknown to anyone but Vito. And sometimes it seemed not even he knew what he'd stuffed in there. He was a bit older than Richie, but his still black hair grew thinner by the day, and his hairline receded deeply. His face was overly fleshy, and his eyelids drooped so badly his nearly black eyes were scarcely visible. He could look intimidating, but he was the softest one of the three. Finally, he mumbled, "You know it's child's play."

"That's what I'm afraid of." Richie sneered.

"Knock it off, Richie." Shay snapped with a twist of his mouth. "You know we'll handle it."

There were times, like now, when Richie wondered just who the boss was in this merry crew. At the same time, he knew Shay had a point. He was acting like an S.O.B., and had no business picking on Vito.

And Shay was the only guy he knew with the balls to tell him so.

Shay was Vito's opposite in every way. With six-feet-three-inches of rangy muscle, he could have passed for a model in *GQ Magazine*. Richie always enjoyed watching women react to him. Everything about him was pristine, and he rarely had a single strand of his light, wavy blond hair out of place. His eyes were large and deep blue, with an almost purplish hue in certain lights. His clothes were expensive and impeccable, and he had a penchant for silk ascots. Even his voice sounded exquisite. But he never allowed anyone to get close. Not women, not men. Richie and Vito were the best friends Shay had, and even from them, he kept secrets.

"You know there's nothing difficult about this case." Shay pressed his fingertips together as he spoke. "Another gambler, no self-control, got in over his head. His nuts are in a vice and he wants us to keep it from his wife. It's scarcely a big deal, and not a problem. The thing that is a problem, however, is you."

Richie's irritation level soared. "Me? You're saying I'm a problem?"

"Exactly," Shay said. "Something's wrong with you."

Richie could scarcely believe what he was hearing. "That's bull shit."

Shay ignored his outburst. "Does it have to do with Mayfield?"

"Rebecca?" Richie widened his eyes. "What makes you think that?"

"You haven't seen her the last two nights, and if you don't tonight, *Saturday night*, no less, that'll make it three. What's going on? Did you two get into a fight again?" Shay asked.

"Hey, I pay you two to spy on other people, not on me. It's none of your damn business whether I see Rebecca or not."

Shay folded his arms and leaned back in the chair. "It's our business when it makes you a bastard to work with."

"You know we care about you, boss," Vito added. "Whatever it is, you can tell us. Did she dump'ya?"

"No!" Richie smarted. At least, he didn't think she had. But he knew something was bothering her. When he called, she was always "busy." Being Rebecca, she tended to clam up instead of telling him what was going on in that cop-brain of hers.

"Maybe it's time you just go see her," Vito said. "Face-to-face."

"I'm busy here," Richie answered, his arms spread wide.

"You think this place can't run without you?" Shay asked. "Your new manager would walk through fire if you asked him, and you know it."

"Go see her, boss," Vito said. "We can't handle you this way."

Shay stood. "I think Vito's right," he said. "But it's up to you. I'll let you know what I find out about your guy's finances. Maybe he's not as hard up for cash as he wants you to think."

Vito got to his feet, as did Richie. "I'll head out, too, boss. I'll tag after your Mr. Big tomorrow, let you know what I find out." Vito couldn't keep up with Richie's ever-changing clientele, so he tended to use "Mr. Big" as the name of any person whose case they were working.

After they left, Richie sat alone in his office, gave a thirsty glance towards his mini-bar, and thought about Vito's suggestion.

3

R ebecca sat in the Emergency unit's waiting room at San Francisco General.

After finding Kiki unconscious, Rebecca had called 9-1-1, followed by a call to the police, expressing her belief that the apartment was a crime scene for a robbery or an attempted murder. The blood beneath Kiki's head was fresh, and the front door lay wide open. She suspected the attacker must have run out when she pounded on the back door.

When the paramedics arrived, Rebecca grabbed Kiki's purse and cell phone knowing she would need Kiki's health insurance and social security numbers, if not her credit cards. She also picked up her own handbag with her badge and cell phone. Waving the badge, she climbed into the ambulance to go to the hospital with Kiki. One look at her expression and the paramedics didn't try to stop her.

Once at the hospital, as the nurses whisked Kiki off to the trauma center to be worked on, Rebecca caught her breath and phoned Kiki's son, Esteban. From what she and the paramedics could see, Kiki was unconscious as a result of something having been used to strike her several times. They feared her skull had been fractured, and that such a blow could lead to potentially fatal bleeding and swelling of the brain.

Rebecca was distraught about her friend's condition, but managed to sound calm and assuring for Esteban's sake. As she sat waiting for him to arrive, and waiting for word from the doctor's about Kiki's condition, she couldn't help but remember when she first met the boy as a gangling teenager of sixteen. Kiki once told her he'd developed a major crush on her, but once he started dating girls his own age, the crush had vanished as quickly as it had begun. Now twenty-two years old, Esteban was a recent graduate from San Francisco State University in computer sciences. He lived with a couple of roommates, working as a barista until a decent job came along in the tech industry. In the meantime, Kiki gave him money when needed.

Esteban found Rebecca in the waiting room. She had not yet been given information about Kiki's condition from any doctor. After talking to Rebecca, he had called his older sister, Sierra, who was living in San Jose. She was now driving to the hospital as well, and should be there in a couple of hours.

All they could do was to wait. After about five minutes of waiting, Esteban decided to avoid conversation and find solace on his cell phone. He had turned into a handsome young man, Rebecca noted, with long black hair and a surprisingly muscular build. She knew Kiki worried about him not being able to find a good job and was afraid he might give up looking if his jobless situation went on too long. The last thing Kiki wanted was for him to decide that making fancy lattes and living on his mother's dime was all that life would ever hold for him.

Rebecca found the latest copy of *People* and was about to sit back down to read it when, from the corner of her eye, she noticed movement. She looked up to see Richie storm towards her like someone hopped up on too many of Esteban's high-octane espressos.

"Why are you out here?" he raged as he neared. His dark eyes studied her, his expression simultaneously relieved and angry. "Don't tell me you're still waiting to see a doctor? What's wrong with this place?"

The others in the waiting area looked up at the handsome but irritated fellow wearing a black suit, white shirt, and unknotted black bow tie. From his clothes, Rebecca knew he had come here straight from Big Caesar's, but she wondered why. She took his arm and pulled him away. "What are you doing here?" she whispered.

He studied her with confused eyes. "What am I...? I heard about you, about the ambulance. What's going on?"

"I don't know yet. The doctor's haven't told me a thing. But there was so much blood. I know head wounds bleed a lot, but—"

"Wait. Whose blood?"

Now Rebecca was the confused one. "Kiki's. She was attacked in her home."

He ran a hand through his hair. "Christ Almighty!"

She noticed that people nearby were staring as if trying to hear what was being said, and even the Esteban stirred a bit. "Let's go outside."

They stepped onto a small outside patio set up primarily for smokers. There, he put his arms around her. "God! I was afraid ..." He pulled her close.

"Afraid of what?" she asked, breaking away.

Dark eyes met hers. "I left work early and decided to stop by your place. I haven't seen you much lately. But I no sooner got out of my car than that old fart who lives next door and sits at the window all day long stuck his head out and told me you weren't home. He said you went off in an ambulance. I came straight to Emergency and found you sitting there." He looked her up and down. "Apparently unhurt and"—he grinned —"looking good."

She glanced down at the fluffy slippers, sweat pants, and bulky top she'd changed into after work. "If you were worried, why didn't you phone me?" she asked.

"If I was worried? If? I was told you were on your way to the hospital in an ambulance. I didn't think they'd let you chat on your cell phone. It so happened, I was scared half to death by the news." His lips tight, he paced in a circle, one hand on the back of his head. "For cryin' out loud, Rebecca! Who knows what could have happened to you? What with the crazy people —killers—you chase after! Of course I was worried."

She tried to look dismayed, but despite her earlier thoughts about possibly, or probably, ending their relationship, she was glad to see him. And the thought that he had dropped everything and rushed to her side thinking she might be hurt, got to her. As she looked at him, she could all but feel her demeanor, her stiff expression, soften, and even she could hear the warmth in her voice as she said to him, "I don't know what to do about you. But thank you for coming."

"It's okay," he murmured. As they half-sat on the balcony railing around the patio, he wrapped an arm around her back. "So what's going on with Kiki? What happened to her?"

She didn't move away. After feeling so scared and worried about Kiki, she appreciated the comfort he offered. Somehow, just having him there made her feel more confident the doctor might have good news. She knew it was ridiculous to feel that way, but there it was.

When she finished her story, he stood upright and paced. He was never one to sit still for long. "I can't imagine anyone wanting to harm Kiki," he said. Then, his face filled with worry, he added, "Are you sure she was the victim? What if someone was looking for you?"

She folded her arms. "Well, that's reassuring."

He flung his arms wide. "I'm not here to reassure," he bellowed. "I want to be sure you're safe. That you've considered all the possibilities. And Kiki being mistaken for you is a very likely one, if you ask me."

She shook her head. "I'm five-foot-ten, blond, and in good physical shape if I say so myself. Kiki's five-foot-two, with long, black hair and a roundish body that never saw the inside of a gym. I simply do not see anyone mistaking the two of us."

"Unless it was someone paid off to go after you. You know your apartment is well hidden. What if it was someone who was told to go after the woman who lived in that building?"

"Just stop, Richie. I don't need you to make me any more paranoid than I already am."

"You aren't nearly paranoid enough," he shouted. "Look, I'll get Shay and Vito to look into—"

"No, you won't!" she said, wondering why, with him, she so often ending up in a shouting match. It was another reason this relationship was for the birds. As for Shay, she was sure he was a former CIA sniper, a former hit man, or possibly both, before he started working for Richie. And Vito—although he was a sweetheart—was also, at best, muscle.

She drew in her breath and tried to calm down. "I'm sure it wasn't a mistake. Someone went after Kiki. Not me."

"You know it was no burglar," he said. "When confronted by a homeowner, they run. They don't bash anyone's head in."

"Unless the guy was crazy or on drugs," she added. "But all the lights were on. Anyone would know the flat wasn't empty."

"So if whoever broke in wasn't trying to rob the place and wasn't after you, then going after Kiki with a hammer or whatever, hitting her in the head that way, leaves only one conclusion. Someone wanted her dead."

She didn't even want to think about what he was suggesting. "I can't imagine that."

"Any idea how he got into her flat?" Richie asked.

"I don't know."

He put his hands on her shoulders and waited until her gaze met his. "I'm sorry to say," his voice smooth as melted butter, "but it still makes more sense that you might have been the target."

She studied him a long moment, then took a deep breath and stepped back, breaking his hold. She put her hands on her hips. He was upsetting her on several, very different, levels. "All this tells me is that I'd better go back home and talk to the cops who showed up at her house to see what they're finding."

"What cops? No one was there when I arrived." He looked at her a long moment with the same worried, unhappy expression he'd worn since he first showed up at the hospital.

She couldn't believe what she was hearing. "What do you mean, no cops? It's a crime scene."

"Oh?"

Frowning, she called Bradley Frick, the landlord. He had been talking to the police when she left for the hospital with Kiki. Bradley confirmed what Richie told her—the police had already come and gone. No one was there, and no one was watching the place.

Bradley did not sound happy about any of it.

She put in a quick call to the patrol officers who had first shown up. After talking to them, she was even more disgusted.

"Great, just great," she said to Richie. "The uniforms at the scene called it in to the robbery detail. But since it appeared that nothing was actually taken, Robbery is questioning if it's really their case. Maybe it's a simple assault, they said, which could be handled by Central Station."

"Do they have the manpower?"

"Not as much as Robbery." Her shoulders slumped. "I know what's going on. Our new police captain is monitoring crime statistics and clearance rates down to the performance of individual inspectors. Word is out that each unit needs to improve the clearance rates of their cases, which means everyone only wants cases that are easy to solve."

"Bureaucrats," Richie muttered.

"I've got to go back home and see what's going on," she said, and then remembered that she didn't have her car. She glanced at Richie. "Um..."

"No car?" he asked.

She shrugged. "I didn't want to leave Kiki."

They went back into the waiting room and she gave Esteban her phone number, making him promise to call her as soon as he was given any news about his mother's condition. He nodded and returned to Twitter.

"Let's go," Richie said, draping his arm across her shoulders and giving a light squeeze of support. "I'll drive you."

4

R ichie had finally reached the point in his life where he rarely did things he didn't want to do. But that freedom didn't include dealing with his mother. Around noon the next day she phoned him.

"Nothing's wrong, Richie," Carmela Amalfi said. "But I need you to come to my house right away. I mean, fast. Now, in fact. It's about my friend, Benedetta. I want you to talk to her. She needs advice, and I can't help her."

"What kind of advice?" he asked. A reasonable request in his opinion.

He heard her suck in her breath. He knew what was coming even before she said, "It's complicated."

And that was the kiss of death for any argument he might have. "Complicated" to his mother had a mystical significance. Anything complicated couldn't be discussed by phone, email, text, or god-forbid, by mail. Anything complicated must be handled face-to-face, and depending on the severity of the issue, either over a cup of coffee (mildly severe) or a glass of wine (big trouble).

He knew if he didn't do what she said, drop everything and go to her house immediately, he'd be hounded until he complied. The best way, no, the only way to get her and Benedetta—whoever she was—off his back was to do whatever Mamma Amalfi asked. And so he found himself driving in circles near the top of Russian Hill searching for a place to park. Normally, he pulled into the space in front of his mother's garage, but another car was already parked there. The troublesome Benedetta's, he guessed. It didn't make him any more eager to help her.

Still, he guessed doing this was better than sitting home thinking about Rebecca. He was sick of worrying about her. Last night, hearing she had been driven off in an ambulance, nearly killed him. It brought back the horror he felt when he got a call about his fiancée having been in a car accident. He had rushed to the hospital back then, and sat in some depressing, ugly waiting room for nearly two days. They couldn't save her.

One part of him wanted to run from Rebecca, to stop seeing her or caring about her, so he could stop worrying about her and the dangers of her job. But another part wanted to run to her, to make the most of whatever time they might have together. Having lost his father at a very young age, and then his fiancée whose job was in a bank, he had learned that life threw curve balls that were completely unexpected. It was crazy that someone like bank loan officer could be taken at an early age while some daredevil Flying Wallenda type could live to a hundred. But such was life.

And life was also too short to spend looking for a parking space in the city. He pulled into an opening in front of a garage just a few doors down from his mother's flat. He hoped he'd hear the tow truck before it drove off with his Porsche.

Carmela lived on the top floor of a three-story building that

Richie had bought for her when he couldn't convince her to move to a nicer, larger home. She refused to leave "the old neighborhood" and the friends she'd made there. A tenant, a middle-aged single man, lived in the flat below, and a garage took up the ground floor. Richie had only seen the tenant once in all the times he'd gone there to visit his mother. Either the guy worked all the time or purposefully avoided him. Richie suspected it was the latter. But if Carmela liked him, he didn't care.

Richie let himself into the main door and hurried up the interior staircase to Carmela's flat. He knocked, then opened her door. "Ma, it's me," he called.

"*Vieni qui*, Richie," she answered. "In the kitchen."

He walked in and his gaze immediately went to the table. The wine was out. *Uh oh.*

Carmela introduced him to Benedetta Rossi. She was in her sixties and "skinny as a rail" to use one of Carmela's expressions, with dark brown hair and eyes. To him, she resembled most of Carmela's friends, except that her nose was long, thin, and shaped like a beak. He took off his jacket and sat at the table with them.

"Vino?" Carmela asked. The wine bottle was nearly empty, and looking at the flushed cheeks and shiny eyes of both women, he knew why.

He asked for coffee. Since Carmela always had a pot going, she immediately poured him a cup, and then added some slices of coffee cake to the cheese and sourdough bread already on the table.

"So what's going on?" he asked, hoping to get this over with as soon as possible. Earlier that morning he had heard from Rebecca that Kiki didn't need surgery "at this time," and was resting, but he wanted to be available to her in case Kiki took a

Again, Carmela answer. "They extended the kitchen— made it bigger. And put in laundry room for her."

"Did they add new plumbing or have a plumber do it?"

"They did it," Benedetta said. "Just a few pipes.—*Ma che schifoso? How this such*—How hard is that? And a bigger water heater, of course."

"Of course," Richie said, wondering how he was going to get out of his. It sounded like a first class screw-up. "And the electricity? Did they deal with two-twenty wiring for the dryer?"

"Two-twenty?" Benedetta looked at Carmela. "How am I supposed to know all that stuff? They put in a plug. Several plugs. What's the big deal?"

"That's not good," Richie muttered.

Benedetta stared so hard at him, if her black eyes could have leaped across the room and smacked him in the head, they would have. But then, her lower lip started to tremble, and her eyes grew watery. If she began to cry, Richie knew Carmela would feel obligated to join in.

San Francisco did have a stringent and expensive building permit process because of earthquake and other potential dangers, real or perceived, and frankly, as a way to put more money in the city's coffers. As a result, building inspections and permits were a hassle that no sane person wanted to get involved with. "Usually, you can work things out with buyers," he said. "They might be willing to ignore the issues if you give them a credit in the sale price. Then they can fix them themselves."

"Not this problem." Benedetta's voice was low and the tone bitter. Her mouth wrinkled. "The building inspector said he might have to turn it over to the building compliance department, and that they might condemn my house!"

Richie could scarcely believe her. He'd never heard of a building inspector going that far—especially in an area where homes sell for well over a million dollars. "How long ago was all this work done?" he asked.

"Let's see, it was when my Georgie was still living at home. He was twenty-five when he got married, and now he's forty-three, so about eighteen, twenty years."

"And in all this time it hasn't given you any problems?" Richie asked.

"None."

That was another surprise, albeit a pleasant one.

"Did you tell him that?"

Benedetta nodded. "I was in tears so he gave me the name of a realtor who deals with distressed property. Distressed! Who knew my house would be called such a thing?"

Carmela patted her friend's hand and pushed some coffee cake towards her.

"Did you talk to the realtor?" Richie asked.

Benedetta snorted, then took a bite of the cake with perfectly sized, obviously false, teeth. Richie waited until she swallowed. "Yeah." She took a sip of wine. "She said she might be able to sell it to some foreign investor with a lot of money who won't care if he has to tear it down and build something else. I was ready to go for it until I talked to Carmela."

"That's right." Carmela faced Richie and tapped the side of her nose. "I can smell a scam a mile off, and this one stinks to high heaven. I've been to Benedetta's house many times. It's a beautiful place, worth a fortune. There's nothing wrong with it."

Richie pondered his mother's words. She might drive him crazy most of the time, but she was crazy like a fox when it came to anything involving money. If she smelled a rat here, she might be right. And, if Benedetta's house went at a "distressed" sale price, considering its location, he might be interested in it himself.

"I'll check it out," he said. "And I'll look into the realtor you're dealing with. I want to see how legitimate she seems. What's her name?"

Benetta dug through her gigantic handbag and then gave him the woman's business card: Audrey Poole, Bay-to-Breakers Realty.

Oh, shit.

He not only knew her, but when he bought and sold real estate, he used to date her. If Audrey was involved, this might not be a good situation for a number of reasons.

5

Rebecca arrived at Homicide early that same morning. Although it was Sunday, she wanted to use the quiet of the day to finish paperwork on a few old cases. The first thing on her agenda, however, was to phone Esteban for an update on Kiki's condition.

Last night, Esteban had given Rebecca the news that Kiki had regained consciousness. Now he explained that the CT scan had showed some swelling inside her head. They inserted an intracranial pressure monitor in the space between the skull and the brain to monitor any changes in pressure. If it increased, she would need surgery. The important thing was to keep her calm and still.

Her second order of business was to call up Robbery and find out why they weren't all over Kiki's apartment trying to find out who attacked her. Okay, she knew why. But that didn't mean she was above trying to shame someone in the department into investigating what had happened.

Richie phoned Rebecca and asked about Kiki's condition and then asked Rebecca to dinner. She told him she was too busy and quickly ended the conversation.

When she left work, she headed to the hospital.

She was glad to find Kiki looking amazingly alert, despite her bandaged head and the brace she wore to stabilize her neck and spine. All kinds of tubes were stuck into her arms and head, as well as taped to her skin to monitor her. Given all that, Rebecca realized if Kiki had been struck another time or two, she most likely would be dead.

Her son and daughter were with her. Rebecca said hello to Esteban and then hugged Sierra, who she hadn't seen in several months. Sierra was a beautiful young woman, twenty-four years old, now working as a paralegal at a Silicon Valley law firm. Kiki once mentioned that Sierra was finding the job so interesting, she was thinking about going to law school. Kiki was quite proud of her daughter.

"Kiki, how are you doing?" Rebecca said softly.

"I'm going to get better, Becca. And when I'm out of here, I'm buying Spike a filet mignon. My kids told me it was his barking that caused you to check on me."

Rebecca nodded, proud of her little guy. "He'll love it."

The room was filled with a number of small bouquets of flowers, and another that was a dozen roses. "Look at that," Rebecca said to Kiki. "It appears you have an admirer."

"I wish," Kiki murmured. "He's actually your admirer. Those are from Richie."

"That was nice of him." She went over to the flowers. Their soft scent took away some of the medicinal hospital smell of the room and gave it a gentle perfumed quality. She lightly touched a rose petal as her thoughts momentarily turned to the man who sent them.

"I don't know when I'll get an admirer again," Kiki said. "They shaved off most of my hair!"

Rebecca took a deep breath and turned back to Kiki with a smile. "You'd get admirers if you were bald."

Rebecca sat by the bed, and after more talk about how Kiki was feeling, Rebecca gently prodded her about the night she was attacked.

"I know you're a cop, Becca," Kiki said. "And you've got to talk about these things, but I didn't see who attacked me. And I have no idea why he did it."

"Do you remember anything about it?"

"Only that, one minute, I saw you and Spike in the yard, and the next some man was standing in my kitchen."

"Did you recognize him at all?"

"No. He wore something over his face, and gloves, I think."

She wearily shut her eyes and Rebecca waited a moment before she said. "Do you remember anything else?"

"I fought ... and I ran. And I think ... I think I heard you calling me."

Rebecca nodded. The story confirmed what little she had heard from the investigators after she'd kicked up enough of a fuss at work that they sent someone to Kiki's flat. They had dusted it for fingerprints, but they hadn't found any that were on file. It went along with Kiki's statement that her attacker wore gloves.

"Can you think of any reason someone might have a grudge against you or want to hurt you?" Rebecca asked.

"You think someone is after me?" Kiki's breathing started to quicken.

Her daughter, Sierra, put her hand on Kiki's arm. "It's okay, Mom. She's just looking for a motive. Nothing to worry about."

"Sierra's right," Rebecca chimed. "I'm just thinking of someone who had a big bill to pay, or something like that. Someone who's angry and things got, momentarily, out of hand."

Kiki drew in a deep breath. "I don't know. My head hurts so much." She shut her eyes again.

"Okay," Rebecca whispered. "Don't worry about it. We'll have plenty of time to talk later, when you feel a little better."

"One thing ..." Kiki's voice was scarcely a whisper. "The owner of the building, my spa's building, he wants to sell. I have a good lease, so they can't force me out. I spent a lot of money converting the space into a spa ... they can't force me to go ..."

"Who wants to buy it?" Rebecca asked.

"I don't know. Some foreign investors. One of my customers knows all about it. She's a realtor."

"Let me look into that."

"It's not a reason to attack a person, is it?"

Rebecca had worked any number of cases where a person was brutally attacked for a lot less reason than ruining a real estate deal. And in hers, the victims had ended up in a morgue, not a hospital. "I'm sure we'll find yours was a random attack—a robbery gone bad."

"Maybe," Kiki murmured.

Rebecca didn't want to trouble her any more than necessary, but she had to ask. "There were no signs of a break-in at your house, and your alarm didn't go off. Did you, by chance, let someone inside?"

She saw that Kiki was asleep. She faced Sierra and Esteban. "If you can find out the answer to that question, let me know. Maybe she let him in and just doesn't remember."

The two nodded, still somewhat shell-shocked at seeing their strong, vibrant mother in this condition.

"Let me look into a few things. First, who's the owner of the spa's building?"

"I don't know," Esteban said.

"I'll text it to you," Sierra said, flipping through Kiki's phone. "Here he is. Winston Young."

"Thanks," Rebecca said. "And what's the name of the realtor involved?"

"I'll have to look through my mom's clients for that," Sierra said. Esteban shrugged.

"What's happening with the spa?" Rebecca asked.

Again, Sierra answered. "It's closed today—Sunday—so it's no problem, and I already called and left messages canceling everyone's appointments for tomorrow. That's how so many people know Mom is in the hospital." She gave a nod towards the flowers. "After tomorrow, I'll have to see how much Mom's assistant can handle. I'll stick around to oversee things until Mom is able to go back to work."

"No, you have your own work," Kiki said, half opening her eyelids. "And my client's name is Audrey Poole."

Rebecca, Sierra, and Esteban looked at each other and realized that even under heavy medication, Kiki still wanted to be included.

"I'd better go," Rebecca said softly, "before the doctors throw me out."

Despite the fact that earlier that day when Richie asked Rebecca to dinner, she said she was too busy to go, he expected she went to visit Kiki after work and that, as a result, her "dinner" would consist of leftovers, a salad, or something from a fast-food line.

By nine o'clock at night, he figured she would be home from the hospital and probably hungry. He picked up a pizza—pepperoni, sausage, mushrooms, and black olives, their mutual favorite toppings—and drove to Mulford Alley. Her SUV was parked atop the red-zone that covered one entire side of the narrow street. Everyone who lived in the alley parked that way. For some reason, meter maids never entered it, so the cars didn't get ticketed.

He parked behind Rebecca and used the key she gave him to

let himself into the breezeway to the backyard. When he reached her apartment door, however, he knocked. Somehow, that seemed like the right thing to do.

She looked surprised to see him. He guessed she was expecting her landlord, the only other person, besides him and Kiki, with easy access to her apartment door. "Richie? But I thought I said—"

"I suspected you might be hungry, being so busy and all." He lifted the pizza box closer and could tell the moment she caught a whiff of it. Her eyes lit up, she swallowed hard, and then nodded. He knew all thoughts of turning him away vanished.

"Come in," she said.

"I figured you might have gone to see Kiki instead of eating much for dinner." He walked straight to the coffee table and placed the pizza box on top. Her apartment consisted of two rooms: a small bedroom with a bathroom off it, and a larger room that held the living area, a small dining area, and a kitchen divided from rest of the room by a counter. Somehow she had managed to make the small space homey and comfortable with a variety of cushions and quilts in warm colors.

"Hello, Spike," Richie said. The dog had run up to greet him. Richie petted him. "I've got something for you." He pulled a doggie toy in the shape of a massive green caterpillar out of his pocket and put it on the floor. Spike pounced and immediately began to chew on it.

Rebecca put plates, napkins, red pepper, and Parmesan on the coffee table, but her expression was troubled. Richie tried to ignore it. "Any wine or beer?" he asked.

"In the fridge."

He opened the door and saw an unappetizing half-eaten burger covered with plastic wrap. He'd guessed right about her dinner. He grabbed a couple of Dos Equis.

"Thanks for the pizza," she said as she dished out a slice for each of them. He sat on the sofa, but instead of sitting next to him as always, she took the rocking chair beside it. "I guess I am hungry."

Rebecca filled him in on Kiki's condition as they ate the first slice. "A name came up that you might know. One of Kiki's clients is a realtor."

"There are a gazillion realtors in the area. I hardly know any of them anymore," he said.

"This one's name is Audrey Poole."

A bite of pizza seemed to lodge in his throat. He coughed it free. "Yes. Her, I do know." He sipped some beer, thinking he might not want to let on just how well he had known Audrey. "But," he quickly added, "it's been a long time since I last saw her. A very long time."

Rebecca gave him a strange look. "Interesting." She picked up a second slice of pizza and bit into it.

As Richie did the same, memories of Audrey came to mind. They had dated some ten year earlier.

Where had the time gone? He'd been making money flipping houses throughout the bay area. When he had enough to get banks to give him big loans—apartment-building size—his whole life changed. The risks were greater, but that meant the rewards were a lot better. He couldn't believe how the money started rolling in.

During those heady days, he met Audrey, and they started dating. She had been attractive back then, quite attractive. She was fun, kind of crazy. She was from New York, which anyone could tell as soon as she started to speak, and she'd come to San Francisco because she'd heard about its booming real estate market and figured that since she had managed to do well in cut-throat New York City, she could make a killing in a more laid-back city like San Francisco. She had a terrific head for business, always trying to find a good deal and new ways to work the system. He would never forget one of the last times he'd talked to her. He had called to ask her out, and she said she couldn't go because she was too busy selling the property she owned.

"You're selling property," he repeated. "So what else is new? You're always selling and buying. What's the big rush? You need cash or something?"

"No, Richie. The market's turned. Time to get out while I can."

"Not in San Francisco," he insisted.

"Even here. Trust me."

"You're not kidding?" he asked.

"Do I kid about money? Do I ever? Anyway. I got to sell five buildings this week."

"Five?"

"See why I don't have time to play? But if you don't believe me, maybe you want to buy one."

"No thanks, Audrey," he said. "I believe you."

"Good. Now get off my phone." With that, she hung up.

He took her advice and sold just before the city's real estate market crashed. Now, it had recovered, but he would have lost his shirt if he hadn't listened to her.

He talked to Audrey a couple of times after that, but then she started dating someone seriously, and so did he, and since he was no longer in real estate their paths rarely crossed. He did hear about her from time to time, and from a distance he kept tabs on her because that was the kind of businessman he was. But they hadn't spoken in years.

"Richie, hello-o-o." Rebecca's head was cocked as she looked at him, as if she suspected where his thoughts had wandered.

"Sorry. I was just thinking about the time I was heavily invested in real estate. It was nerve-wracking. I'm glad to be out of it."

"Was she your agent?"

"God, no. My cousin Caterina would have killed me if I didn't keep the commissions in the family. But I'd talk with her a lot."

"Sounds as if you liked her."

"Yeah." He couldn't help but smile. "She had all kinds of experience."

Her eyebrows rose.

He noticed he had finished his slice of pizza and took more as he tried to explain. "When I was doing real estate, she was really good on the big picture. Much better than me. I owe her."

"Audrey Poole, savior," Rebecca said.

He couldn't help but remember what it was like being around her. "Yeah, I'd say so."

"You used to date her, didn't you?"

He nodded. "There was never anything special between us, but she was a fun person."

"Much more so than a serious cop, I suppose." She said the words with a smile and a lilt in her voice, but he caught the solemn undertone.

"I happen to like serious cops."

She took another bite of her pizza.

He needed to change the subject. "I just remembered. I hear she used to date one of your old boyfriends. Maybe still does, come to think of it."

"Who?"

"Sean Hinkle."

Rebecca's eyes narrowed. "That was ages ago. How would you know about him?"

Oops. "I don't remember. His name came up one time. I don't know why. Anyway, I hear he now works somewhere in the mayor's office."

Rebecca's gaze was like cold steel. "So, she dated both you and Sean. I have to meet this woman."

"I don't know if she's particularly serious about Hinkle. Were you?"

"You're kidding, right?" She pursed her lips. "What do you know about Audrey Poole's business?"

He wondered why she changed the subject away from Hinkle. Maybe she cared more about him than he'd heard. But how could she think twice about a guy with a name like Hinkle? He could imagine what kids did to it: Sean Tinkle, Sean Hickey, he could go on. And if they had married, she would be called Inspector Hinkle. He shuddered. "What do you want to know about it?"

"Kiki's landlord wants her to give up her lease so he can sell the building. It seems Audrey Poole might be involved somehow."

"You think Kiki stood in the way of Audrey making a big sale?"

"So I understand."

"Whoa, that's a scary thought." He remembered Audrey putting the screws on people. She was one tough cookie. "I'll see what I can find out."

"Hmm." Rebecca's face was filled with curiosity at his reaction.

Another thought crossed his mind. "Is everything okay at Kiki's spa?" he asked.

"I think so. Why? Her daughter said she called and canceled all the appointments for today and tomorrow."

"Did anyone check on the place?" he asked.

Rebecca's eyebrows rose. "Oh, my."

She phoned Kiki's son, Esteban. "I'm just wondering if you or Kiki's assistant or any police went to the spa today to make sure everything's okay there."

Rebecca's conversation was short. When she hung up, she

faced Richie and shook her head. "No one has been there all day. I'm going to meet Esteban and check it over."

He stood. "I'll drive you."

"No need."

"Whose idea was it?" he insisted. "And who brought over the pizza which is almost all gone, by the way."

She nodded. "Let's go."

K iki's spa, the "House of Beauty," was on Union Street near Fillmore, a convenient location for wealthy customers from Pacific Heights or the Marina district to reach. Rebecca knew she could have refused to let Richie come along with her, but the truth was, this wasn't her case, and she had no more "right" to be there than he did.

Besides, she couldn't help but think that if she went through with her plan to stop seeing him, this was perhaps the last time she'd be with him looking into some possibly dangerous situation going on in this city. She had to admit that as much as she enjoyed being in Homicide, those cases that she worked with Richie were definitely among the most interesting of her career. As she sat in his Porsche, she breathed in the smell of the leather interior, and the spicy masculine fragrance of the aftershave and hair gel that he wore. She knew those scents would always remind her of the days and nights she had spent with him.

"What?" he asked, giving her a quick glance. "You're looking at me oddly."

"Nothing." She turned her head to peer out the window and

tried to concentrate on the street instead of the man beside her. As they rode down Union, she was surprised at how many businesses had already closed for the night. Parking was easy to find, a rarity in San Francisco.

She had given Esteban strict orders not to enter the building alone. He stood by the front door as she and Richie approached. She introduced the two men. Esteban was about to use his key to unlock the door when she stopped him and tried the doorknob.

The door opened, unlocked. Not a good sign.

"But how?" Esteban mumbled, confused.

"Where's the key pad for the alarm?" she asked.

"Inside, to the left." His eyes were wide.

"Let me go first." From its special compartment in her handbag, she lifted her service weapon, a SIG Sauer 229. "Wait here."

Esteban quickly nodded.

She slowly entered the building, listening for any sound, and looking for any indication she wasn't alone—except for Richie. She didn't waste her breath demanding he wait with Esteban. One glance at his expression and she knew it wouldn't happen.

All was quiet. Richie reached for the light switch before she did, and she gave him an okay to turn it on. A comfortable reception area lit up, with cushioned chairs covered in a pastel blue fabric, and pale walls done in a faint lavender shade. Past the large reception desk were the salon and then a number of smaller private rooms. She saw no movement, heard no sounds, and witnessed no uninvited stranger scurrying for cover.

She motioned for Esteban to enter. He hurried to the keypad. "The alarm's already been disarmed," he whispered.

Also not good, she thought.

"The office is at the end of the hall," Esteban told her.

"Wait here," Rebecca ordered as she began a search of the main room where big chairs with the foot tubs sat, along with counters covered with zillions of nail polishes, and little cubicles where they did the eyebrow feathering and Botox injections.

Richie not only didn't listen, he was doing his own search.

Along the hallway to the office were four private rooms where body wraps and mud baths were done. At each, Rebecca perused the room.

"I don't like the looks of that," Richie said, suddenly right behind her as she opened a door and switched on a light.

In a mud bath room, a sheet covered one of the tubs.

She crossed the room and drew back the sheet. A moment passed before she understood what she was seeing. A body was in a mud-filled tub. The mud appeared to have completely dried.

Only the victim's head remained above the surface. But the upsetting part, the most horrible part, was that the entire head, including the hair, had been covered with something resembling a thick gray mud pack. Where the face should have been was a solid gray mask.

Rebecca immediately phoned Lt. Eastwood and explained the situation. She didn't need any official pronouncement from a medical examiner to know she was looking at a murder. Since she was friends with the owner of the spa where the murder took place, she wanted to give Eastwood the chance to assign it as he wished.

Eastwood told her to take charge, and that he'd make all the necessary contacts to get her some assistance. Rebecca was almost surprised by his willingness to take care of routine details. It was almost as if he was glad to have something to do.

"It sounds like my favorite dick, Bill Sutter, will be here

soon," Richie said after she hung up. "I think I'll leave before he arrives."

"No you won't," Rebecca said.

"What do you mean? I want to see him as much as he wants to see me."

"This is a crime scene now," Rebecca said. "You said you wanted to come here with me, so you're going to be processed along with the rest of us."

Richie grimaced, but helped as Rebecca did a quick search of the rest of the spa to make sure no one was hiding in it, and to search for anything that might tell her who the victim might be. She found no one, and nothing.

They then joined Esteban in Kiki's office.

Rebecca faced him. "Is there any stored information about the alarm system?" she asked. "We know it was disarmed when we got here, but I'd like to know when it was last armed for the night, and what time it was shut off."

Esteban opened the program that controlled the spa's security. "Hey, this is strange. The system was never turned on yesterday after work. It looks as if my Mom didn't put it on when she left for the night, and she always did that."

"Can you tell what time Kiki left?"

"No. It's not that sophisticated."

"Why wouldn't she have set the alarm?" Richie asked.

"She would have. She usually locked up the place," he said. "Although sometimes, if her assistant had a late appointment, my mom would leave and let her lock up. She trusted her. Also, a night crew comes in around seven to clean up everything since absolute cleanliness is important in a day spa."

"That's some top-notch cleaning crew if they didn't notice a body in the mud bath," Richie muttered, clearly unhappy at being stuck there.

Rebecca asked, "Do they clean those rooms every night?"

"Absolutely. The tubs, too," Esteban said, then corrected himself. "They're supposed to, anyway."

"I know a guy who once owned a spa," Richie said. "He had cameras in every room so that if anyone was accused of becoming a bit friendlier than appropriate, there was proof one way or the other."

"My mom has cameras like that, too," Esteban said.

"She does? That's wonderful!" Rebecca said. "Let's take a look."

Esteban knew how to work the system and pushed a few buttons on the computer, expecting videos to show up on the monitor. "Uh, oh."

"That doesn't sound good," Rebecca told him.

"I don't know what's wrong." He tried several more steps without luck. The video screen stayed black. "The cameras were turned off and everything on them wiped clean."

"I knew it was too easy," Richie said. "Whoever broke in here knows a lot about how this spa operates. Almost like an inside job, or something."

"True," Rebecca said. She couldn't help but wonder if the robbery investigator who thought Kiki knew someone, or something, and wasn't saying, might be on the right track.

Just then, there was some noise at the front door. The crime scene investigators had arrived.

7

Several months back, when Richie was working with Steve Burlington on a messy 'situation' involving his wife and his mistress, he had learned that everyday around noon, Burlington could be found sitting at the bar of the Comstock Saloon on Columbus near Pacific Avenue. Now, Richie entered the bar and, right on schedule, there sat Burlington.

Richie liked the Comstock. With its massive hundred-year-old bar and antique furnishings, it looked like something out of the Barbary Coast days when San Francisco was a rough-and-tumble Western town, not the chichi place it was today.

He hadn't really wanted to go to a bar in the afternoon, but he needed something to help him put Rebecca out of his mind for a while—and the bar's "White Lily," an old-time Comstock drink made of gin, rum, orange-flavored curacao, and absinthe, just might do it. Looking for Burlington gave him an excuse to get one.

Richie took a seat next to Burlington. They greeted each other with jokes and jabs in the way of a couple of old friends in a bar. Only after catching up was over, and Richie took a sip of his "White Lily" did he bring up the reason for his visit.

"I heard that you're selling your Third Street office building to some foreign investors," Richie said. "I've come across a couple other situations, too, with foreign investors. What the hell's going on?"

"Why? You interested?" Burlington asked. He was a beefy fellow with a blond pompadour-shaped toupee, expensive clothes, and wearing a pinky ring with an ice-cube size diamond. A real one. He made sure the ring caught the light as he reached for his drink.

"Maybe," Richie said, shifting his arm so that his Piaget watch could be seen. "Sounds like a lot of money is coming into the city."

"You got that right. I tell you, Russian and Middle Eastern money, including Iranian, were big, but now Chinese money is absolutely flooding this area. You got any junk you want to unload, this is the time to do it. I thought the goddamned Commies weren't supposed to be rich, but these guys are Saudi-prince kind of wealthy. I don't know what's going on, but if they want my for-shit white elephant out on Third, I'm more than happy to unload it. And I'm getting a good price."

"So I've been hearing," Richie said, growing increasingly interested. "How do you find the buyers?"

"The crazy part is they goddamn found me," Burlington said with a laugh. "I mean, holy shit, was that luck, or what? Apparently, they need to go through a broker of some kind. In my case, I use a realtor who works out everything. I mean everything. You should give her a call. Her name is Audrey Poole."

Richie drew in his breath. He could scarcely believe it. She always said she wanted to corner the market. It seemed she had —the very lucrative foreign investment market. "As a matter of fact, I've tried to reach her a couple times today. But her phone goes to voice mail. I tried her office, but same thing is happening. Do you know if she still lives in a condo up on Pacific Heights?"

"You know about that place, huh?" Burlington gave him a broad, knowing smile. "Very few do, from what I understand."

"We used to be pretty good friends," Richie admitted.

"I'll bet you were. I've heard she still lives out that way. I never had the pleasure of seeing it first hand, myself."

"Good," Richie muttered, remembering the troubles this guy had when his mistress threatened to tell his wife about their $800,000 love nest unless he signed it over to her.

Burlington laughed and slapped Richie on the back, apparently having similar flashbacks. "Anyway, I know that she often flies to China. She likes to convince buyers in person to use her offshore holding company as their investment vehicle. Maybe she's not answering because that's where she is."

Now, Richie was impressed. "Offshore holding company? You're shitting me."

"Hell, no! That's how foreign investors from 'not-so-friendly' countries get their money out of their country and then become property owners here without having to deal with our laws. When you get how it all works as a money machine, you'll be amazed. Like I said, it might even be something you want to get into. On the side, if you know what I mean."

Richie was taken aback by the legal outlandishness of such a scheme. He didn't know Audrey had it in her. "I'll look into it," he said. "That's for sure."

∼

Rebecca stood in Dr. Evelyn Ramirez's laboratory waiting for the autopsy to begin. Both Homicide and the ME's space were in the Hall of Justice building. Rebecca spent more time than she would have liked down in the basement laboratory since Bill

Sutter claimed he had a weak stomach, which made it difficult for him to watch bodies being cut up. She was, therefore, the team's "designated observer." This autopsy was even more crucial than most because it should allow her to identify the victim.

Last night at Kiki's spa, as soon as possible, she had the CSI team process Richie's fingerprints and then sent him out of there. She didn't want him and Bill Sutter to face each other. The blood between them wasn't simply bad, it was curdled.

After filling in the crime scene unit's Inspector Pacheco, Rebecca returned to Kiki's office where Esteban waited.

There, she tried to reach Kiki's assistant, Inga Westergaard, but her phone went to messaging. Rebecca asked her to call as soon as possible.

She then turned to Esteban. "Let's go back to the cleaning service," she said. "I don't understand how they could have missed the body." He found the company in the computer system.

Rebecca phoned Evergreen Business Cleaning, and spoke to the owner. Jerome Gleason was filled with curiosity about what had happened at Kiki's place and asked Rebecca nearly as many questions as she did him. He also wondered when the spa would again open up.

Rebecca told him what little she could and then asked what conditions were like at the spa Saturday evening.

"I don't know. We weren't there."

"I thought you went every night it was open."

"Usually, we do, but I got a call not to show up at the usual time."

"Who called you?" Rebecca asked.

"The assistant, Inga."

"Are you sure?"

"Oh, yes," Gleason said with a bit of a sigh in his voice. An amorous sigh, truth be told. He then added, "I'd know that accent anywhere. She said she had a late customer, and she'd call when the spa was free so I could fit it into my schedule. But she never called back. Then yesterday, Mrs. Nuñez's daughter called and told me the place would be closed until further notice."

Rebecca thanked him for his help.

"Does that make sense to you?" she asked Esteban after relaying all she was told.

"Not at all."

"Show me the appointment screen," Rebecca said. "Let's see who that late night customer was, if anyone."

Esteban opened the appointment software. At the end of the day, only one appointment was shown.

It belonged to a person Rebecca had heard glowing words about from Richie: Audrey Poole.

Shortly after that, Bill Sutter had shown up, immediately followed by the medical examiner's team. Rebecca quickly filled both in on what she'd discovered.

Dr. Evelyn Ramirez and Rebecca had worked so many cases together, they were becoming friends. They had gone out a few times for coffee or, after a particularly sad or ugly case, something stronger. Ramirez was an attractive woman, in her fifties, and divorced. It gave Rebecca pause when she looked around at the people she worked with and found that nearly all had either never married or were divorced. It didn't say good things about the compatibility of her chosen field and married life.

Dr. Ramirez left the detectives to check on the body, but seconds later she called them back to her. "I need to speak to you both right now," she said, standing beside the corpse. "This body is completely covered with dried mud. It's hard as concrete."

"Yes, we know that," Rebecca said, wishing Ramirez didn't have the ability to make her feel like a misbehaving child.

"I'm not taking the mud off here," the ME announced.

"But we need it off to find out who the victim is."

"I have no idea what the mud might be covering that's loose or potentially volatile, or what evidence it might contain that could be lost or contaminated in this environment. I won't do anything until I have the body and the mud surrounding it lifted out of the tub and delivered, intact, to my laboratory."

Rebecca and Sutter glanced at each other, then Rebecca said, "But once there you'll take the mud off tonight, right?"

"No. It's far too late. I want to think about the best way to approach this." Ramirez lifted her chin. "I've never had a situation like this before, and I want to make sure I don't do anything that will cause problems later. Removing it should be like removing the caste for a mask."

Rebecca hated the death-mask image the words conveyed.

As the ME's group carried off the body, and CSI did what they could to collect evidence—and there was an amazing amount of DNA-containing substances throughout the spa, including hair and nails and dried skin flakes—Rebecca phoned Sierra to tell her what was happening.

The two of them felt it would be best not to tell Kiki about the body at that time. The doctors wanted her to remain as calm and possible, and a death at the spa, particularly not knowing who had been killed, would be upsetting, to say the least.

Now, some sixteen hours after the body had been found, the ME finally began to remove the dried mud. Ramirez decided to begin with the head, and to cut along the edge of where the face should be, and then to lift off the mud pack. That should have resulted in a neat, clean removal. Unfortunately, it didn't work out the way she'd hoped, and she ended up having to pick crumbling pieces of gunk off the woman's eyes, and to all but dig it out of her mouth, nose, and ears.

The process, Rebecca had to admit, was stomach-turning. She found it more unnerving than a typical autopsy, which she had learned to watch with a studied, professional eye.

But even before the face was completely revealed, Rebecca recognized the woman.

She now understood why Kiki's assistant, Inga Westergaard, had not returned her calls. She had met Inga the two times she'd gone to the spa for a massage and mud bath. The memory of it, given Inga's death, gave her a cold chill.

From the autopsy, Rebecca learned that Inga had died by being smothered to death by the facial mud having been stuffed into her nose and mouth. Someone must have really hated her. She had struggled, but bruising on the head, chest, and arms showed she had been overpowered. Rebecca couldn't help but connect the blows to the head Inga that received with those of Kiki. Same *modus operandi*, same perp, was a common finding.

The body was fully clothed under all that mud, and there was no sign of sexual assault.

Dr. Ramirez would perform blood work and other analyses, and if anything of note turned up, she would contact Rebecca.

Ramirez believed Westergaard had been dead nearly thirty-six hours. That meant, Rebecca realized, her death took place around the same time as Kiki's attack.

8

After hearing about Audrey Poole's offshore holding company, Richie was more eager than ever to talk to her. He called several more times with no luck and she hadn't returned his messages. He didn't like being ignored, stiffed by an old "associate."

He also called Bay-to-Breakers Realty numerous times. Once, a receptionist actually answered. She said she didn't know when "Ms. Poole" would be back in the office and took a message.

He went to Audrey's condo. No answer. Her neighbor said she hadn't been there for a couple of days. That gave him an idea of where he might find her, but first he had to take care of another pressing problem.

The day before, after visiting his mother, he had driven Benedetta Rossi home. She was a bit too looped from Carmela's wine to drive herself or even to take the cable car. He was afraid she'd topple off, and then he'd have to listen to Carmela lamenting her friend's accident every time she'd think about the word "cable" let alone "cable car." It would be more than he could handle.

But one look at Benedetta's beautiful home from the outside made him want to see the inside and its remodel for himself. The house had been built in the 1920's, and retained most of the original, ornate woodwork. The kitchen and bathrooms were dated, but the house had been decently maintained over the years. It didn't even show very many earthquake cracks, and they were visible in just about every older San Francisco home.

He couldn't see anything seriously wrong with the house, not even in the basement or the garage. Benedetta showed him the building inspector's report, and sure enough, it claimed her foundation was cracked and rotting. But how could the inspector have known that? He looked at the man's name, hoping he was someone Richie knew from the past. Darryl Kreshmer. Never heard of him.

The more Richie looked over the house, the more interested he became in the property and in questioning why this woman was being leaned on to sell it as "distressed" to foreign investors.

That morning, Carmela had called to ask about his progress on Benedetta's permit problem. He promised to report back soon. He knew she would keep bugging him until he took care of it, so he contacted the Department of Building Inspections on Mission Street and asked to speak to Darryl Kreshmer. He set up a meeting that very afternoon.

Now, he drove to the building inspection office. Soon, a mountain of a man came out to meet him. A massive hand reached for his. "Mr. Amalfi," Kreshmer said. "What can I do for you?"

"I'm representing a woman whose home you recently looked at. Benedetta Rossi. Francisco Street."

"Yes. I remember. An old house, beautiful neighborhood," Kreshmer said. As he nodded, his double chin flapped against his chest.

"It's also a very nice house," Richie said. "I understand you went there to inspect the installation of a new furnace and ended up telling her that a remodel done years ago was no good."

Kreshmer folded stubby fingers over his bulging stomach. "That's right. She had no permits. It was done by an unlicensed relative, from what I understand. When I look at it, I can't tell if it was done right or not. It's got to come down."

"It's lasted eighteen years."

"Dumb luck, Mr. Amalfi. I've been doing this a lot of years. I know these houses like the back of my hand. I also know the neighborhoods. We haven't had a large earthquake since 'eighty-nine. One big shake and who knows what will happen to that house. Nothing has been secured as it should be. The pipes could break, the electricity could short out, and the water heater is attached to an illegally installed gas pipe. You know what that could do in an earthquake? It could destroy the entire block. It's very, very serious. I suspect there are other problems as well. It's always the case when we start to open the walls and foundations of these old houses. Considering the owner's age, I also doubt the place has been kept up as it should be."

Richie had wanted to play nice, but something about the bureaucrat's smugness made him want to pop him in the mouth. "All that is pure speculation. It's lasted through several quakes with no problem at all."

"The remodel has to go, Mr. Amalfi. I cannot allow an unsuspecting person to buy that house and then have it come down around their ears. Mrs. Rossi wants to ignore these problems, but she can't. She threw me out of there! Who does she think she is? If she wants to play hardball with me, I'll play right back."

"I'm sure she didn't mean anything."

"Like hell she didn't." Kreshmer's face turned red and glistened with sweat. "She all but said she could ignore me. Well, not on my watch. In some localities, if the buyer doesn't care and wants to fix problems himself, the town or city looks the other way. But that's not how I operate. This one, I just might take to the compliance inspectors."

"I see." Richie was taken aback at the man's vehemence. "I'll have to talk to her."

"Look, she's sitting on a place worth well over a million in today's crazy market." He slid his hands in the front pockets of his baggy slacks. "I'm sure she can find a way to fix it, or find someone who will tear it down and put up something more fitting for that neighborhood. I get it that my report isn't the sort of thing you want people to know about in a neighborhood like that one."

"She told me you suggested a realtor, Audrey Poole."

"I suggested she call 'a' realtor. I don't remember naming any one in particular."

"She said you did. How else did she get the name?"

"How should I know? Realtors are always giving me business cards because of my job. I probably handed her a stack of them. I would never recommend any one in particular."

"You didn't recommend Audrey Poole?"

"Of course not. Why do you keep asking about her?"

Richie didn't answer; he'd have to ask Benedetta more specifically how she got Audrey's name.

"One other thing," Richie said. "Did you happen to inspect some property for sale on Union near Fillmore Street? It's a two-story place with a spa on the ground floor."

"Hmm. A spa out in that neighborhood sounds familiar. Yes, I remember. Some work was done to the spa, and I needed to make sure it met the permit requirements. That was all."

"And did it?"

"Yes. Nice work."

"Was that the only inspection you did on it?"

"I don't remember any other permit requests on the property. But I can look it up."

"No, not necessary," Richie said. "Not yet, in any case. Well, I guess I'll get going. It sure is too bad about an old lady, Benedetta Rossi, not being able to sell. I mean, I understand your position completely. In fact, I was thinking about buying her house myself. I'd fix it up with all the correct permits, of course. That would work, wouldn't it?"

Kreshmer's eyes narrowed, and he seemed to be sizing Richie up. "I don't know. It might cost more than it's worth, unless you want to live there a lot of years."

"I see. Well, I appreciate your advice," Richie said. "I imagine when you see so much money being spent and driving up prices on single-family homes in the city, it's got to be frustrating. I know civil service salaries are small, so let me say, if I go ahead and buy the house, I'd be happy to pay you for your advice on the best way to do the work to get the permits approved."

"No need. It's my job," Kreshmer said.

"But you will have saved me a lot—tens of thousands, probably—and I believe in rewarding anyone who helps me."

Kreshmer's cheeks blazed red. "You can stop right there. I know where you're going. I don't want your money. I'll be keeping a close eye on that place. You can leave now."

Richie didn't get it. Back when he was making real estate deals, paying off a lot of the people involved behind the scenes was practically standard operating procedure. He handed Kreshmer his business card. "If you change your mind, call me."

After Inga Westergaard was identified, Rebecca and Sutter left Homicide. Sutter drove them in his Chevy to Inga's apartment in a poor part of the Mission district. She had three roommates—Destiny, Grace, and Kaitlyn. Two were home. They were in their early twenties, thin and attractive. They were stunned to learn Inga had been murdered. Not until asked did they realize that she hadn't come home the past two nights.

"Where did you think she'd gone?" Rebecca asked.

"Probably to stay at her newest boyfriend's place," Destiny said, and then gave a little giggle.

"Who is that?" Rebecca asked.

"I don't know. She never told me his name." Destiny turned to Grace. "Do you know who he is?"

"Nope, but she was always secretive." Now, both women giggled. Rebecca wondered what that was all about.

"Would Kaitlyn know?" Rebecca referred to their third roommate.

"I doubt it. Inga and Kaitlyn didn't get along. Inga hated that Kaitlyn did a lousy job when it was her turn to clean the kitchen and bathroom. We took turns. Inga was good at it, a real germaphobe. Kaitlyn couldn't care less."

"Inga let her have it," Grace added with a snicker.

"Oh, man, I remember one time." Destiny laughed. "She had quite a mouth when she was unhappy."

"God, but it was so funny!" Grace joined in the laughter.

Rebecca was finding these two almost cruel in their callous disregard for their dead roommate. "When did she start seeing this latest boyfriend?"

"A month or month-and-a-half ago, I guess," Destiny said. Grace nodded.

"Did she often stay out all night?" Rebecca asked.

"A few times. Not as often as Grace," Destiny said. Grace socked her arm and, again, they both laughed.

"Did she ever talk about her job?" Rebecca asked. She glared at Sutter, surprised he was so quiet, but he stared at the brain-dead roommates as if afraid he might catch stupidity germs from them.

"Not to me," Grace said and looked at Destiny.

"Don't look at me. We scarcely said two words to each other."

Rebecca grew increasingly exasperated with twiddle-dee-dum and twiddle-dee-dumber. They stood in the kitchen. Rebecca realized they were in a small, two-bedroom flat. The girls had turned the living and dining rooms into bedrooms so they each had one. "Did she have any other close friends who might know more about her life and her new boyfriend?"

This time Grace answered. "Nope. Just us."

Poor woman. "What about her family?" Rebecca asked.

"They're all in Denmark."

"I'd like to go into her room, look for information about her boyfriend and family. We'll have to call the family and tell them what happened. Do you mind?"

As Rebecca suspected, she could have walked out of there with everything Inga owned for all the attention or concern those two had.

Sutter helped her search. They found information about Inga's phone number, but not the actual phone. It was amazing how people's lives seemed to be lived on their phones these days. Inga's computer wasn't password protected, which Rebecca found surprising considering she shared the apartment, but then Rebecca saw that she received few emails that weren't spam. She did have profiles on Facebook, Snapchat, and Instagram, but didn't post anything much. She occasionally mentioned going somewhere with a male companion. The latest was named "Luke," but nothing else about him had been stated.

Sutter also found a number of names and photos from Denmark in a box in the closet. The people in the photos looked a lot like Inga and were probably her parents and other relatives. Rebecca wondered how difficult it was going to be to find someone who spoke Danish to break the news to Inga's parents. It wasn't a job she looked forward to handling. Death notifications to next-of-kin were another job Sutter didn't like doing and palmed off on his "junior" partner.

Overall, the two of them found nothing in Inga's life that would give anyone cause to want her dead.

Finally, since no relatives were available to identify the body, Rebecca decided to bring both women to the morgue to do so. Maybe, she thought, if they came face to face with violent death, they wouldn't be so disgustingly cavalier about it.

9

The next afternoon, Richie sat across from his mother at her kitchen table. He brought her a box of Napoleons, cannoli, and éclairs from Victoria Pastry in North Beach. It was her favorite bakery shop, and he knew he was going to have to keep on her good side when he gave her his news.

She poured large mugs of coffee for them both, and then split a cannoli and a Napoleon, putting half of each on their plates.

"This is so good, Richie," she said, taking a big bite of the cannoli. "Now, what's going on? I know you didn't bring me all this because you think I'm too skinny and need the calories."

Richie nodded. They understood each other well. "I don't think the building inspector is going to back off. He's furious that Benedetta threw him out of the house. He's insulted. But that aside, do you know how Benedetta found the realtor, Audrey Poole?"

"I don't know. Sometimes these people just show up and ask if you want to sell your house. It happens to me all the time," Carmela said. She now took a bite of the Napoleon. "Mmm. I'm not sure which I like best."

"Is that what happened? Audrey Poole just showed up?"

"It's important?" Carmela licked her fingers. "It doesn't seem important to me."

"It is."

Carmela rolled her eyes, picked up her phone and used her unsticky pinky finger to punch in Benedetta's number. Richie put it on speaker so he could hear both ends of the conversation. Carmela didn't mention the building inspection, but went straight to asking how Audrey Poole entered the picture.

"I phoned her," Benedetta said. "I told her I want to sell my house, but it has some problems, and the building inspector said she might be able to help me."

"So it was the building inspector who told you about her?" Richie asked.

"Yes, of course."

"He told me he gave you business cards from a lot of real estate agents," Richie said.

"What does he know? He gave me a lot of business cards, but every one of them was hers. *Maleduquat'!*" Benedetta's dislike for the man came through loud and clear.

"Interesting," Richie muttered

Carmela then told her the building inspector seemed to be especially angry because she threw him out. "*Non è vero!*" Benedetta's voice quivered with rage. "Not true! He's a liar, that *faccia di katzo!*"

Richie put his hand over his mouth to hide his smirk. Nothing like getting a sweet little Italian lady mad and then hearing her say the object of her ire has a face like male balls. At least it sounded a little less gross in Italian.

"Benedetta," he interrupted as she continued to spew one fierce Calabrese epithet after the other—even more than he understood and he thought he pretty much knew them all. "We're going to have to find some way around this inspector. I'll work on it. The worst case is that we'll need to pay for some permits with a minimal amount of remodeling."

"Permits, hah!" she yelled. "What's with all the permits? I thought this was a free country! Now, every time I turn around, somebody has their hand out. Why are you taking *his* side, that *gornudo!*"

Now she called him a cuckold. "I'm sorry—"

"I never had a problem with my remodel. It meets code. What, you think I'm stupid?"

"No, but—"

Benedetta was all but screaming into the phone. "But nothing! You think I want my house to fall down around my ears now? You can go to hell, too! *Gita schlamorta gita mort'!*" With that, she hung up.

"What did she just say?" Richie asked.

Carmela shrugged and reached for an éclair. "I don't know how to translate it, but the meaning is that you should die spitting blood. She's upset."

"You think?"

Carmela chewed a big bite of éclair and took a moment to ooh and aah over it before adding, "If Benedetta says the work is up to code, I believe her."

Richie didn't know what to believe, except that he didn't like having Calabrese curses flung his way. A part of him still believed in the evil eye. "I'll see what I can find out, Ma."

"Good. And take a cannoli with you. I don't want to get fat."

She put one in a zip-lock bag and handed it to him as she waved him off. Then she turned and picked up the phone again.

As he left, he heard her again talking to Benedetta, and apologizing for Richie's rudeness and lack of understanding.

∾

The day before, shortly after the autopsy, Rebecca had contacted the police in Copenhagen to break the news to Inga Wester-gaard's parents. Now, she and a Danish translator supplied by the SFPD were on the phone with them to answer those questions she could, and to glean any information they might have to help her investigation.

The conversation was draining. It was bad enough doing a death notification in English. Going through an interpreter, she found herself wishing she could add her own words of comfort, but she didn't know how.

When the call to Denmark ended, Rebecca needed to get away from her desk to clear her mind. The only inkling of trouble that Kiki and Inga were in any way connected with was the sale of the building that housed the spa. Richie had sworn that the kind of people Audrey Poole dealt with could be dangerous. Rebecca tried to contact Audrey Poole by calling Bay-to-Breakers Realty but the call continued to go to a message machine.

She eventually tracked down another number for Poole but that one, too, went to messaging. The only address listed for her was the same as the real estate office.

Sutter had gone there several times, but it was always closed. She was thinking she might drive out just to take a look at a real estate office that never bothered to open, but first she had a stop she thought might be more beneficial.

She and Sutter went to the home of Winston Young, owner of the building that housed Kiki's spa. They hoped to get some first-hand information on the status of the sale he wanted to make. The spa took up the entire first floor, and above it, Mr. Young lived with his wife.

Rebecca and Sutter sat in Young's small, cramped living room. The couple was in their late sixties and had lived there for the last twenty years, ever since their youngest child married and left home. "We're investigating Inga Westergaard's death," Rebecca said.

"Oh, yes. Terrible!" Winston Young cried. He was Chinese and of medium height and build. His hair was thinning, but not yet receding. "We're very sad about the death. And the attack on poor Mrs. Nuñez. Kiki is a nice lady. We hope she is doing better."

His wife, Deanna, sat by his side on a bright green loveseat. Rebecca and Sutter sat facing them on a pink sofa. Deanna was shorter than Winston and quite round, with straight gray hair and full, rosy cheeks. Bright eyes looked from the inspectors to her husband, and she smiled constantly, although she didn't say anything. Rebecca was sure, however, that she understood every word and probably didn't miss a thing going on around her.

Rebecca asked a few general questions about them. Winston Young was retired, having sold his trinket shop in Chinatown three years earlier. Finally, Rebecca asked, "Did you hear any noises coming from the spa after hours on Saturday night?"

"No, nothing," Winston said.

Deanna shook her head.

"Did you ever see Inga Westergaard with a young man, a boyfriend?"

"Never," Winston said.

Sutter jumped in at this point. "We've heard you would like to sell this building."

Winston looked nervous and rubbed his hands a moment. "It was a hard decision. We never thought about it, but then our neighbor, Herman Ling, said he was selling his property, the building next door, to some people from China. They have a lot of money over there these days, you know. Herman told me how much he's getting for his place—and it's a dump. I was shocked. It made me curious how much I could get for mine." He glanced at his wife and she gave a slight nod. "When we heard, of course we want to sell!"

"So," Sutter interrupted, "You're saying Ms. Nuñez is holding up the sale."

"For now, but I believe they can convince her to move in time. Probably, in this city with all the safeguards for renters, it will take a lot of time. Much easier would be to buy her out. I don't know why they don't do that."

"I think," Deanna said softly, "they talk to her, but she say it will hurt her business to move now. She getting lots of good customers. She want them to be loyal, and then she will move, and they follow. Now, too soon."

Winston chuckled. "Deanna likes to gossip. Don't listen to her. I don't know what's been said. All I know is, I'm ready to sell and move to someplace like Walnut Creek, where our oldest son lives. It's warmer there, too. I told Kiki she needs to make them increase their offer and then take it."

Deanna looked at Winston with a frown.

"But," Winston added quickly, "whatever is happening with the sale, I don't believe it's the reason that young girl, Kiki's assistant, was murdered. The people who want to buy are in China ... or, so I've heard. I can't believe they would harm Kiki, let alone kill anyone over a piece of property. That would be wrong and bring very bad fortune to the property. Chinese owners would know that." He gazed with stern eyes at Sutter and Rebecca. "No Chinese connected with this sale would want to see anyone die in a building they were going to buy."

Sutter glanced Rebecca's way. "Could be," he murmured.

She didn't know much about Chinese ways. There weren't many Chinese where she grew up in Idaho. Richie grew up near Chinatown and she suspected he could tell her if that was true or not.

She really had to stop relying on his help.

She and Sutter thanked the Youngs for their time and soon left.

Clearly, the two weren't seeing eye-to-eye on this. But it gave Rebecca something to work on.

She tried again to reach Audrey Poole, but received no answer.

She realized, of course, that someone who had once dated Audrey very likely might have a private phone number, and might even have a home address. She wasn't thrilled about asking for his help again, but it was her job to look at everything.

For the sake of her investigation, she would contact Richie.

Or so she told herself.

10

W hat the hell's going on, Hinkle? Cops talking to our sellers? Driving by Audrey Poole's business? Leaving messages for her? How close are they getting?"

Sean Hinkle's fingers tightened on his phone. He hated being yelled at. "We've got to simply sit tight. They have nothing that will connect with us."

"Too many questions are being asked. I heard one of Audrey's sellers was being pumped about how the whole system works. I don't like it."

"I'm sorry. If you want me to try to stop them from going any further, I'll do it."

"Stop them? Of course I want you to stop them. What are you, some kind of moron?"

"Yes, sir. I mean, I will stop them, sir." Sean wanted to hang up, but he didn't dare.

"One woman's dead. That can scare people off. You need to talk to the reporters. The newspapers need to say that the dead woman found at the spa died by accident. She fell asleep while taking a mud bath. And then, I want them to drop the story. You got that?"

"Yes, but I'm not sure how I'm supposed to know anything about a murder investigation."

"I just said it wasn't a murder. You're on the mayor's staff, aren't you?"

"Of course, but—"

"By the time the cops or anyone else is ready to make a statement that it was murder, no one will care or remember. You got that, Hinkle?"

"I've got it."

"It needs to end now."

"Yes, sir."

"Maybe she's gotten too big."

"She?"

"Audrey Poole."

"I don't think it has anything to do with her," Sean said, his voice soft and timid. "I'm sure it doesn't. And I'll stop the questions from being asked. The story will go away."

"It had better."

11

At dinner time, Richie sat across from Rebecca at one of his favorite restaurants, The Jade Dragon. He'd been stunned when she called and suggested dinner tonight.

He had brought Rebecca to the Jade Dragon the first evening they spent together—last Christmas Eve. He never dreamed back then that he and Rebecca Rulebook—which was how he used to think of her and, come to think of it, still did—would continue to be together several months later.

Since today was the 24th of the month, it was, in his mind, an anniversary of sorts. But he would never admit anything so sappy to Rebecca.

He knew she was upset about Kiki's attack and busy working on Inga Westergaard's murder—still trying to find the woman's boyfriend as well as a motive for her death. But beyond that, he hoped that tonight he would find out what was bothering her.

The main floor of Jade Dragon was always noisy with small tables and booths along the walls and larger, round tables suitable for families with children in the center. The ambiance was happy and colorful—the walls and ceiling were festooned with posters and a variety of masks and objects depicting Chinese dragons and other mythological creatures. Its bright lights and packed tables caused tourists who filled Chinatown to take notice and wander inside, adding to the crowd. Thanks to Richie's friendship with the owner, Benny Wong, Richie and his guests were always brought downstairs to a peaceful dining area with soft lighting and private tables. There, they joined the Chinatown elite. Waiters appeared almost instantly, and so did the food. Richie enjoyed selecting a variety of dishes, but always included a bowl of beef won ton soup and an order of pork chow mein, which he considered staples of any decent Chinese meal.

"You've been busy," he said to her after they'd sat and gave the waiter their order. "I've hardly seen you."

"Yes," Rebecca said. "It's Kiki. I cannot believe what happened to her, and then her assistant's death. It's all hit me quite hard."

The stilted way she spoke wasn't the Rebecca he was used to.

"I'm sorry to hear that," he said. "At least Kiki is doing well."

She dropped her gaze and shook her head. "A couple of hours ago, her daughter told me some sort of fluid had built up in her head and they had to perform surgery. The doctor hopes he caught the problem quickly enough that there'll be no consequences from it."

Richie covered her hand with his. "That's tough news. I'm sorry to hear it."

She pulled her hand free. "It's a setback. But if all goes well, she'll be fine."

Their soup was served. When the waitress left, Richie said, "I've got interesting news. One of Carmela's friends wants to sell her house. It's a beauty and on the north side of Russian Hill. It has some 'permit' problems, but I'm thinking I might be able to get it at a good price."

"You'd move?" she asked.

"And live that close to my mother? I don't know, to tell the truth. I suppose I could always flip it."

She nodded. "I see. I also found out a little about the sale of the building where Kiki's spa is."

"Oh?"

As they ate, she then launched into her meeting with Winston Young, Kiki's landlord. Again, with the shop talk, he thought, acting as if he were her supervisor and she was giving a report.

He thought she'd have been more interested in him wanting to buy a big house, the sort that could be a nice family home.

"I was thinking," she said, "about your comments about Audrey Poole. I'd like to talk to her, but I can't reach her, which is very strange with her being a realtor and all."

"It is," he said. "She's not answering my calls either. I was told she might be out of the country."

Rebecca raised her eyebrows. "You've been trying to reach her?"

He swallowed hard. "She might consider herself the agent for the house I was telling you about. I'm not sure. And I want to find out what she knows about its structural issues."

"Of course," Rebecca said. "And so, do you have a better phone number for her than the one at her office or the one she uses online? Or, maybe, her home address?"

"You're stuck?" he asked.

"Yes, and I hoped that you—"

"So that's it." He pushed out his lips. "I was wondering why you finally wanted to have dinner with me. I hoped it might be my boyish charm. Guess not. What's going on Rebecca?"

The waitress served the rest of their meal. Rebecca didn't answer until they were alone again. "I just thought you might have some suggestions on how I can reach her, that's all."

Richie put some *kung pao* chicken on his plate. "I'm not

exactly having any luck myself, you may have noticed."

She frowned. "Oh, well, I suppose I could try Sean Hinkle, if you're right that he's dating Audrey Poole."

"Oh yes, your old flame. How could I forget? I wonder how he's doing," Richie said as he reached for the *moo goo gai pan*.

"I guess I'll find out. Just like you'll eventually reach Audrey Poole."

His jaw tightened. "Then we'll both be happy."

Rebecca's hand stilled a moment over the chow mein. "I see." She then continued to put some chow mein on her plate.

Richie put down his chopsticks. He knew he was wading into dangerous water, but he had to know. "Would you go out with him again if he asked?"

"Sean?"

"Who else?"

She seemed to carefully choose her words. "We only dated a short while, and I soon found I didn't care that much for him. I don't see that changing." She took a sip of tea. "But since you mention it, I'm sure you meet women all the time you'd like to go out with."

He knew better than to answer a loaded question like that. How dumb did she think he was? He picked up his chopsticks and pushed the chicken around on his plate, weighing his answer. There wasn't any good one. "Since *I* mentioned it?"

She grimaced. "I'm not joking."

"You have to bring this up before I even take a bite of the *kung pao*?" he muttered. "It's one of my favorite dishes. Thanks loads."

"Fine. Forget what I said." She began to eat.

Nothing like taking a woman out to dinner on an anniversary of sorts and have her talk about dating others. The chicken didn't taste nearly as good as he remembered. "Is this really about people we used to date, or is there more to it?"

She pressed the napkin to her lips then took a deep breath. "Sometimes,"—her voice was soft and low—"sometimes I wonder about us."

"Aah. So that's what this is about." He was almost relieved. This, he could handle. So typical, go out with a woman a few times, and she's thinking about a wedding ring. He should have known. "You want some sort of commitment." He reached for his tea.

"No, I don't."

He felt as if an ice cube had been dropped down his back. Her words didn't make any sense to him. Women don't talk that way—not in his experience. Hell, in his experience, they didn't even think that way. Then, he got it. "Okay, Rebecca. What did I do?"

"Do?"

"You know. What did I do that's making you talk like this? Did I forget something important? It's not your birthday is it?"

She folded her hands, then lifted sad and troubled blue eyes to his. "The truth is you confuse me. *We* confuse me. I care a lot about you. And I know you feel the same. But when I think about 'us' all I see are our differences. And I don't know what to do about them. Sometimes, I think the smartest thing for both of us—for both—would be to simply walk away."

He carefully placed the chopsticks on his plate, his appetite completely gone. She wanted out. Okay, he knew it would happen eventually. Maybe just not this soon.

He was a big boy. He could handle it. But, still, he couldn't help but ask, "Is that what you want?"

"Not really." She sounded disappointed, somehow. He didn't get her; not one bit. But then she asked, "Do you?"

Something about the way she looked at him, about the tone of her voice, told him how upset she was and how much, despite all that, she cared about him. He was struggling with how to reply when the restaurant owner, Benny Wong, hurried over to their table.

"Richie, my friend," the man bellowed. "They just told me you were here."

Richie was all but speechless, caught between Rebecca's announcement and his old friend's exuberance. "Hello, Benny." He half-rose from his chair as they shook hands. "You remember Rebecca Mayfield?"

"Of course, I do." Benny gave a bow as Rebecca said hello to him. He glanced back at Richie with a big smile. "I don't mean to disturb you, but something has come up that's very strange. But could be very profitable as well. It almost sounds too good to be true, so when I heard you were here, I told myself, 'Talk to Richie.' I've got to know what you think."

"I see. Well, uh ..." Richie glanced at Rebecca. Thoughts of the conversation they were just having gave him a cold chill, but he needed to hear what she had to say. Was it over between them ... or not quite?

Benny glanced at Rebecca, suddenly flustered. "Oh, so sorry, Richie! I don't want to interrupt your dinner. Maybe just one minute? At most, two?"

"It's fine," Rebecca said, then her eyes found Richie's. "Listen to what your friend has to say."

"Thank you, thank you!" Benny all but sang the words. He grabbed a chair from an empty table and spun it around so it faced them. He sat and proceeded to talk about some people in China who were buying up a lot of property in San Francisco using offshore holding companies. Benny wondered if he should join some of those investors.

"I have heard about those things," Richie said. "In fact, I have a former client now who's selling an office building to one such company. Do you have any names? That's the best way for me to check out what's going on."

"Yes!" Benny beamed. "As a matter of fact I do." He pulled out a pamphlet written in Chinese and gave it to Richie.

Richie flipped it from one side to the other, not even sure which was the front of the thing. "This doesn't happen to say Bay-to-Breakers Realty does it?"

"Ah? You read Chinese, Richie?" Benny gave a toothy smile. "How did you know?"

He shrugged. "I know a lot about what goes on in this city."

He saw Rebecca roll her eyes at that, but then she asked, "Tell me, Benny, why would anyone in China want to buy property in this city?"

"It's because of Chinese law," Benny told her. "Despite China being a Communist country many people have become quite rich there in the last few years. But they worry about what will happen in the future. San Francisco property always seems to be a pretty safe bet. It usually stays expensive, so it's a good way to park their cash. Their own government can't reach it here."

She nodded. "Interesting."

Rebecca's phone buzzed. She pulled it out. "The security videos I was waiting for are finally in. Places around Kiki's spa around the time of Inga's murder. I should go back to work to view them."

Richie's gaze met hers and held. Then he dropped his eyes and nodded.

"You want to-go boxes?" Benny asked. "I'll get my staff to make them up for you. And no charge for this dinner. I seem to have wrecked it for you."

"No to-go box for me," Rebecca said. "I'm heading back to work. And you didn't wreck anything, Benny."

As they said their goodbyes, Benny's head swiveled from one to the other, finally noticing the tension between them. He didn't say another word.

12

The next afternoon, Richie knocked on the door of a swank hotel located in the city's downtown area just off Union Square.

"Who is it?" A voice with a heavy New York accent called.

"Richie Amalfi."

The dead bolt clicked. Audrey Poole opened the hotel door, peeked at him with one eye, and shut it again. He heard the chain being unfastened, and then the door swung open wide. "Richie, how did you find me?" She was whispering and looked strained and harried. "Get in here. Hurry!"

He entered the room, and she shut, locked, and chained the door again. She had on jeans and a T-shirt, no shoes, no make-up, and her hair looked like she had washed it and let it dry without doing anything more. The years, he couldn't help but think, hadn't been kind to her. And while some women could get away with no make-up, Audrey was one of those who bene-fited from all the cosmetic help she could get.

"What's going on with you?" he asked, waving at the door locks.

"It's crazy. I swear, Richie." She ran her fingers through her medium length auburn hair as if trying to get it to fall somewhat in place. "Who knew I'd be hiding out like this? You want a drink?" She walked to a bottle of Scotch and an ice bucket.

"No thanks," he said. She made a stiff drink for herself. From the fumes around her, it wasn't her first.

The hotel room had a tiny kitchen area—microwave, refrigerator and some dishes and utensils—as well as a sitting area. He went to a sofa near the windows and sat.

"You didn't answer my question, yet," she said, leaning back against a chest of drawers. "How did you find me?"

"You think I forgot that you helped the owner buy this hotel?" Richie said. "Or that we came here after that party when we were too looped to drive home and you told me you could always find a room here as Lucy Magillicutty? I figured if you wanted to hide in this city, this was as good a place as any. And better than most. Turns out I was right, *Lucy*."

She nodded, her mouth pinched and troubled. "If you found me, do you think others will?"

"Who's looking?"

"Damn it all, Richie." She joined him on the sofa and then laid her head on his shoulder. "Things have gotten pretty bad."

"So I noticed." He put his arm around her.

"I'm going to leave the city. I'm just waiting for a couple deals to close, make sure the money's in my bank, and then I'm off to Argentina."

"Argentina?"

"Buenos Aires is doing really well. Lots of Americans going down there, wanting to buy homes and condos. I'll be fine."

"I'm sure you will. But what are you so scared of?"

"That's the thing. I can't be sure. I think it's all about a couple buildings I've been trying to buy. You heard I have an offshore holding company, right?"

"I have. Leave it to you, Audrey."

"Yeah, well, it's a big money maker, let me tell you. Something you should think about, Richie. Really."

"Like I want more businesses to worry about," he said.

She snuggled closer. "Yeah, right, you've always had a head for business. And quick, big bucks. And women, too, you know. Believe me, sometimes, I'm sorry things didn't work out for us. We always saw eye-to-eye."

"That's true," he said. And that was one of the problems. They were both too much into looking at the money side of things and not at the whole picture. Instinctively, he knew living twenty-four seven on the fast track wasn't healthy.

"Maybe we should try again," she said. "Why don't you come to Buenos Aires with me? If nothing else, we'd have a blast."

"I'm sure we would, but I've got a business to run," he said.

"Yeah. I heard about your nightclub. Well, my offer stands, okay? Anytime. You know, so often I wish I had a guy like you. Instead I meet crazy stalkers. And I do mean crazy. Why am I so damned unlucky?"

He chuckled at that, but found himself shifting away a bit. "Why leave here? If all this fear is caused because of a building you want to buy, why not just walk away from the deal?"

"It's not just the one property, but also these investors. So many can be trouble, bad trouble. It doesn't matter what part of the world the high rollers are from. They all have a lot of influence and power in their home countries. They know how to get their way, how to apply serious pressure, or they wouldn't be so rich that they'd be looking for US properties, you know? So 'walking away' isn't exactly in the cards."

"That's not good," Richie said.

"No, it's not. Anyway, my buyers, from China in this particular case, need a lot of space and they want something in the northern part of the city. I found two buildings on Union, side-by-side, and both owners are willing to sell. Perfect, right? But one building has a tenant who won't give up the lease."

"The place on Union Street—the one in the news," Richie said. It all made sense suddenly.

Audrey nodded. "Yeah. I even joined the damned spa to get to know the owner, but she's stubborn like you wouldn't believe. And now she's in the hospital, her employee is dead, and the police want to talk to me. I keep getting calls from some crap homicide detective. She sounds like a first-class bitch if ever I heard one. I don't want to talk to her. I know nothing! I want no part of this."

"And you think your buyers are behind the attack and murder?"

"The buyers are in China," Audrey said. "But there are others involved."

"Who?"

"I'm not sure yet."

"Talk to the homicide detective who's been calling you," he urged. "I know her. She just wants to get a few answers. She might even find out who's behind all this."

Audrey sat upright and faced him, her eyes hollow. "Yeah, sure. Like she can protect me if I talk."

"Protect you from who?"

"Didn't you hear what I just said? I'm dealing with big-time players and God knows who else. I'm not saying a peep, Richie. Swear to me you won't tell her or anybody else where I am."

"I can't do that."

"You've got to! I let you in here. I trusted you."

"I know, but you can't just hide here."

She pondered his words. "You're right," she said finally. "Maybe I can't. Not any longer."

"What are you going to do?"

She stood and paced. "So you can tell your little homicide

pal? What is she, another woman who's all hot for you?"

His anger flashed that she would talk about Rebecca that way. "Not at all."

She spun towards him. "Oh, boo hoo. Richie's upset that I picked on his friend. Well, I don't give a damn. The only one I care about is me. Right now, one person is in the hospital and another is dead. All over some screwed up deal. Do you blame me for being scared?"

"No, I don't blame you at all. And neither would Inspector Mayfield."

"Stop with the Inspector shit or leave."

He took a deep breath and let a moment pass before saying, "Calm down. Listen, if it's not your buyers, could it be a seller who tried to put the screws on the spa owner and over did it?"

"All I'll say is people are crazy, Richie. Bat-shit crazy. That's why I'm getting the hell out of here."

He also stood. "You've got to be talking to someone about this sale. Who is it?"

"It's all done electronically. As long as I get the money deposited in my offshore account, I don't give a damn if it's the devil himself sending it to me. And as a matter of fact, I don't want to know, okay?" she yelled. "You understand now?"

"Where do you even keep this offshore account?"

"Richie, you're driving me—"

"Where?" he demanded.

"I go through a legitimate bank. It's small, but they've handled the set-up for years."

"A bank?" That surprised him. "Which one?"

"Superior Savings out in the Marina District."

Superior Savings ... It startled him to hear the name. Nobody ever said it around him; he still went out of his way to avoid driving by it. His fiancée used to work there.

He kept his expression tight. "I've heard good things about

that bank. I didn't realize they handled anything as complicated as a holding company."

"They do. The income and outgo alone brings them quite a cut in foreign transaction fees."

Something about this bothered him the more he heard about it—although it might have been strictly because of the "Superior Savings" employee who no longer worked there. He remembered it as a friendly place, and whenever he went there, his day would become a lot brighter.

He hadn't been back to it for four years. He forced himself to turn his thoughts back to the problem at hand. "Come on, Audrey. I know you must have somebody besides a bank that you deal with."

She ran both hands through her chaotic hair. "Sometimes I get leads from one of the mayor's staffers who often goes on trade missions to China—it's very important to the port of San Francisco, if nothing else. He gives me names."

"Names of people he's met on those trade missions?"

"Exactly, and sometimes when a buyer has legal issues, he runs interference for me. At times, he's even gotten the city to sweeten the deal, and at other times, I get my buyers to give him an incentive to go the extra mile for them. You know how it works, Richie."

"That I do," he muttered. He remembered how much under-the-table wheeling and dealing some of his transactions required. Having a cohort in city government would have made things run much more smoothly.

"Anyway," Audrey continued, sitting once more on the sofa. "I even hired a girl who's able to translate Chinese for me. I was planning on hiring someone who speaks Farsi, and another who knows Russian. I would have had my own little UN right here in this city. Now, I'll have to learn real estate laws in Argentina. Damn it to hell!"

Richie also sat, but on the opposite end from Audrey. "I suppose the mayor's staffer who was giving you all this assistance is Sean Hinkle."

She eyed him. "You've heard about us?"

"Just a bit. How long you been seeing him?"

"A couple years." She pursed her lips and then gave a one-shouldered shrug. "It's not exactly a love match, shall we say? We're business partners with benefits, if that makes sense." She gave a dry, bitter laugh.

"A lot of that seems to be going around," he murmured. "But I'm sorry to hear things aren't better for you."

"Thank you." She sounded depressed.

He realized he wasn't going to get any more detailed information out of her, but he couldn't pass up asking about Benedetta's house. "It doesn't have the permits, but I met the owner and she said you might help her sell it."

She cocked her head. "You interested?"

"Might be," he admitted. "It could be a good deal."

"If you want it, get it. I'm sure there's nothing really wrong with the place."

"How are you sure? You working with the building inspector?"

"I don't bother with cheap scams, Richie." Her words were indignant. "Not at this point in my life, anyway. All I can say is, if you want it, I don't care. Work it out directly with the owner. Seriously."

He nodded, believing her.

"Like I said," she continued, "as soon as I get money from a couple deals, I'm out of here. Chinese investors, crazy spa owners, and everyone else who's turned my life into a nightmare can go straight to hell."

〜

Rebecca looked up from her desk to see Richie entering Homicide. She felt her whole body go tense. He walked with his usual swagger as if he owned the place, as if last night's unpleasant dinner date hadn't happened, or, he didn't care that it had. He said hello to his cousin's husband, Homicide Inspector Paavo Smith, and Paavo's partner, Toshiro Yoshiwara, and then turned to her.

"Hi." She couldn't get more words passed her lips.

"Hello to you, too." He sat by her desk.

"What brings you here?" she asked. She paused the screen of surveillance videos she'd been reviewing.

He studied her face a long moment, then said, "I want you to know I talked to Audrey Poole."

So this is business, she thought. She felt relieved. "You found her."

"I did." He gave her one of his self-satisfied smiles. He did have a nice smile, she couldn't help but notice, even when he was being annoyingly smug.

"The big news," he continued, "is that something has scared her badly. She's in hiding, and it has to do with the spa."

"What's she scared of?"

"She doesn't know for sure. But something spooked her enough that she plans to move to Argentina."

"All connected to the spa?"

"She thinks it is."

Rebecca pursed her lips. Little of this made any sense to her. "She must at least know who's behind the deal."

"That she does. She's now working in a specialized market. Her buyers are Iranians, Chinese, Russians—you get the picture."

"Not really," Rebecca admitted.

"It's high finances on a global level. In order to make sales, move money, and not get the feds involved, people like Audrey

Poole have found that working with local governments makes the process a lot smoother."

"Local government?" Rebecca was having trouble following all this.

"Pretty sweet, isn't it? Those wealthy people bring money with them—money for all kinds of purposes. Plus, people like Poole can get ten percent to put buyers and sellers together. And sometimes a lot more money than that is handed out to turn the deal into something the feds won't ever hear about. I may look into trying it out myself."

Rebecca's heart sank. Richie sounded far too interested in this new scheme. "So you're thinking about getting involved in Audrey Poole's business deals?"

"Me? No!" When he tried to look innocent, it never worked. "I only looked her up because of Carmela."

She felt a cold chill. She knew Carmela Amalfi only well enough to know the woman considered her completely unfit to be dating Richie. Her number one crime was that she wasn't Italian, and second, that she was a cop and once "got Richie shot," to use her expression. "Why is Carmela involved? Was she reminding you that you should have stuck with Audrey?" The words were no sooner out of her mouth than she could have sunk through the floor.

"Jealous?" he asked with a definite lilt in his voice.

"You wish!" He looked so ridiculously pleased at the thought she couldn't help but smile, despite herself. "Okay, tell me how Carmela's involved?"

"She isn't. Not directly. But she has a friend who is, Benedetta Rossi. She owns the house I was telling you I might buy, and Audrey Poole is her agent."

"Maybe I need to talk to Benedetta Rossi," Rebecca said.

"Don't waste your time. Trust me on that."

Rebecca did, unfortunately. But she asked him to tell her

everything about Carmela's friend, including her address.

"Let's go back to foreign investors and city staffers," Rebecca said when he finished. "It does sound like big money and shifty deals. And you did mention Audrey dating one of the mayor's staffers."

"And some of these foreign players can get very tough, very fast," Richie added. "Kiki's attack still worries me, okay? You've got to be careful."

"I'm always careful," she said. But then, the more she thought about what he was saying, she couldn't help but shake her head. "I'm afraid, Richie,"—she took a deep breath—"I'm afraid the one who isn't careful is you."

"Me?" He sounded taken aback by her vehemence. "What brought this on?"

She couldn't help herself as all her weariness, worries about Kiki, and frustration about her roller-coaster emotions where Richie was concerned—not to mention worrying about him—bubbled over. "What are you doing looking into foreign investments and heaven-only-knows what kind of intrigue dealing with parts of the world that want to do us harm? Why get involved with them?"

He seethed. "I'm not involved with them!"

"Not yet," she snapped back. "But I know you. I see the gleam in your eyes when you talk about all the money passing hands. And possibly, Benedetta Rossi's house can be a foot in the door."

"I never said—"

"You don't have to!"

"Good Christ, woman! After all we've been through, you still don't trust me?"

"I do trust you. It's the people you deal with I don't trust!"

"Which means you're questioning my judgment."

"Not at all. It's that I know—I see every day—how easy it is for good things to go bad, and for good people to get mixed up in things they never intended to be involved in. And I see the deadly consequences of that happening. It worries me. You worry me."

He glared a long moment, then, his voice tense but measured, said, "Okay. I'll admit there's a lot of money involved. I mean, a hell of a lot. And I deal with people who have money. What do you want me to say?"

She rubbed her forehead, then could only whisper, "I just don't know."

"You see the worst of people in your job. I get that. But you either trust me or you don't."

Arguing was getting her nowhere. It never did; yet it often seemed that was all they were capable of. "As I said, I do trust you and your judgment."

He leaned close enough that, despite everything, she was drawn to him like a magnet. He placed a warm hand on hers, reminding her how much she liked the feel of his hands. Her breathing quickened. "Then trust when I tell you," he said, his voice low and velvety, "to be careful. Your investigation could upset people you don't want to upset."

"Warning taken." She turned away from him and quickly started the surveillance video running once more. She forced her attention on it instead of the man much too close to her.

Richie stood, his mouth a rigid line, his eyes hooded as he peered down at her. "Audrey suggested I go to Argentina with her."

She kept her eyes on the screen. "Well, I'm sure you and Evita will have fun there."

"Oh, yeah. I'm sure we would."

She refused to face him again.

He turned and walked out the door without another word.

She couldn't stop herself from looking up to watch him go.

13

Sean Hinkle's phone buzzed. He picked it up and saw the number the caller used. He didn't want to answer, but he also didn't want the caller to have to phone him back. That never ended well. He took the call. "This is Sean."

"I warned you, but you wouldn't listen, would you?"

"I'm sorry, I—"

"It's too late for 'sorry,' Sean, my friend. Much too late. Audrey's old pal found her, and soon the cops will, too. I'm sick to death of them, always sticking their noses into my business. They're going to screw this up not because they're clever, but because they aren't. They're bunglers, just like you. And that's why you need to fix this mess."

"But the cops—"

"Are only people, my lad. People that can be bribed. Although in this particular case, I don't know that I'd even attempt it, not from what I've heard about the homicide detective in charge."

"You mean Bill Sutter?" Sean asked.

"He's about as much in charge as Howdy Doody when

someone lets go of the strings. Do something about *her,* you idiot!"

"I'll see what I can do."

"And remember, you can't trust Audrey Poole anymore. If she opens her mouth, we're all in trouble. She's dead to us now, not to mention dead weight and a liability. Nothing more."

"I understand."

The line, to Hinkle's relief, went dead.

14

The insistent ringing of her cell phone woke Rebecca from a deep sleep. She opened one eye and looked at the clock. 5:00 A.M.

She wanted nothing so much as to ignore the phone, roll over and go back to sleep. Last night, she'd stayed in Homicide, first going through video from street cameras and local businesses, but none caught the doorway to the spa, and then going through Inga's bank accounts and phone records.

Nothing gave any hint as to why the woman was murdered. Her latest boyfriend, Luke, remained a mystery. Rebecca tried contacting him, but his number had been disconnected. That was suspicious, but aside from him, Inga seemed to live the life of a young, attractive single in the big city. Her friends were her age, her emails and social media posts were about dates, men, movies, music, and money—which she seemed to be perennially short of.

Around eleven, Rebecca gave up for the night and went home.

She soon went to bed, but couldn't sleep. Thoughts of Richie kept going round and round in her head. Ever since they met, she had watched him perform a constant balancing act, almost like walking a tightrope between legal and illegal. Too many times already, she had found herself holding her breath around him, afraid he might topple off that rope and land on the wrong side of things.

Her supervisors had said in not so many words that she would have a very hard time moving up in her career as long as she was involved with him. And her instinct told her to closely guard and nurture the career she had chosen.

She tossed and turned, thinking of all the clever words she wished she'd said to him to get him to see things her way. But no matter how often she replayed the scenario, it didn't make things any easier between them.

Finally, exhaustion must have overtaken her because she remembered seeing 1:30 a.m. on the clock, but nothing more until her phone rang some three-and-a-half hours later.

She dragged herself out of bed, made a travel mug of strong coffee, saw to Spike's needs, and went on her way. In a city filled with a number of rough neighborhoods, gangs, and drugs, it was rare for her to be sent to the tony Pacific Heights area.

It was still dark as she reached a residential street filled with police cars and on-lookers. The street was so steep that cars weren't allowed to parallel park for fear of their brakes not holding. She introduced herself to uniformed officers Dunn and Benton who had been the first to arrive and had secured the crime scene. Dunn, the spokesman of the two, was a large man, middle-aged, with what used to be called a "beer belly." He had a heavy-jowled faced that could either smile warmly or give a hard, icy stare when needed. He was the type of guy she often saw in a policeman's uniform when growing up in Idaho. In San Francisco, many of the officers were female, young, and a lot smaller and thinner. And probably eschewed doughnuts for wheatgrass juice.

"A couple garbage collectors found her," Dunn said, his voice low and gruff. A woman's body lay on the sidewalk, and crime scene tape now blocked off much of the surrounding area. "First, they figured she was some passed-out drunk, but then they considered the neighborhood and wondered if she'd fallen and was hurt. One of these 'sanitation engineers' as they call themselves, walked over to check on her, and when he saw all the blood, he called nine-one-one."

"Where are they?" Rebecca asked, trying to figure out why the garbage truck wasn't still there at the scene.

"They couldn't wait—swore they'd be fired if they didn't finish the route. And with the new chief's policies, I couldn't demand they stay here. But they promised to come back. I've got their names and phone numbers."

Rebecca nodded. They were all under an edict to be a "kinder, gentler" police force, one that would receive no complaints from the public. The new captain had a "zero tolerance" complaint policy. Like that was going to work. "Did they touch anything?"

"They swore they didn't."

As Dunn was speaking, the photographer and medical examiner arrived, and then Rebecca's partner. While Bill Sutter continued to question Dunn, Rebecca went to greet the ME.

"Can this street be any steeper?" Ramirez swore as she made her way to the body. Even at five in the morning, she was dressed to kill, including high heels that made balancing on the hill questionable.

"Be careful," Rebecca said. She wore her usual jeans and low-heeled boots. "You don't want to get hurt out here."

"At least I've got my own ambulance and EMT's," Ramirez pointed out. "They could pick me up and wheel me to safety."

"But if they let go, you'd roll down these hills right into the bay."

"Not funny, Mayfield. My guys wouldn't let anything happen to me."

They wouldn't dare. Rebecca knew the ME had a tendency towards tyranny in her realm. In everyone's realm, come to think of it.

As they talked, they approached the body and Rebecca got her first good look at the victim. Even in death it was clear the deceased had been a beautiful woman. She was medium height, medium build, probably in her early forties, tastefully made-up and well dressed in a cashmere coat, wool dress, and Prada shoes. The uniforms had already told her that they couldn't find the woman's handbag, wallet, and cell phone.

Bill Sutter soon wandered over to see what Dr. Ramirez had to say as she examined the body.

The cause of death appeared evident given the location of the deep knife wounds in the vicinity of the heart and stomach. The murder weapon, however, wasn't anywhere near the body.

"Any idea as to time of death?" Rebecca asked. It was now almost six in the morning.

"I'd say four, five hours ago." Ramirez bent over the body looking for anything strange or inconsistent with the obvious conclusion of a death by stabbing and blood loss.

"So around one or two in the morning," Rebecca said. This location was only a couple of blocks up the hill from Kiki's spa. That would mean investigating two bodies found two blocks from each other within a four-day time frame. If this was a coincidence, considering this was the kind of neighborhood that didn't see many homicides at all, it would rank somewhere up there with getting struck by lightning. She had to consider that she'd been looking at Inga's death all wrong, and the murders were connected to the neighborhood and not the people involved. But then, she reminded herself, Kiki wouldn't have been attacked in that scenario. Could all this mayhem be random, unrelated?

She shook her head. Nothing made any sense. She expected it would become clearer once this woman was identified.

Dr. Ramirez stood. "I'll be better able to determine the time of death after the autopsy. Can I take the body now?"

Rebecca saw that the photographer had finished filming the victim and surrounding area. She glanced at Sutter, who nodded his okay. The ME's staff moved in to transfer the victim to a body bag.

"Our vic looked pretty ritzy," Sutter said to Rebecca as they walked away and looked over the area.

"Ritzy?" Rebecca said with a smirk.

"You know what I mean. Why would someone like her be out here alone that time of night? Her type usually takes a cab. Or a limo."

Rebecca shrugged. "Maybe she's been seeing someone and tonight they broke up so she had to go home alone. It happens." She could have kicked herself. Why did she come up with such a piece of romance drama, and why say it out loud?

"I'm guessing she lives nearby," Sutter said. "It could have been an interrupted robbery. She's still got her rings, earrings, and necklace. They look like gold, and I don't mean gold-plated."

"But her purse is gone," Rebecca said.

"Maybe she put up a fight, and whoever attacked her got scared and ran."

Rebecca frowned. "Did you notice her fingernails? They were long and fake. They would have popped off in any kind of struggle. But if she didn't fight ..."

"That means someone just walked up and stabbed her," Sutter said, finishing her sentence.

"Which suggests this was no random robbery," Rebecca said.

"Perhaps she knew her killer. Whoever wanted her dead might have taken the handbag to throw us off."

Sutter nodded. "Let's see what the people standing around have to say, if anything."

Rebecca and Sutter began talking to the neighbors who were out in the street or watching from doorways. At the same time, uniformed officers were dispatched to search for the murder weapon and any identification the woman might have had.

None of the police were allowed to go knocking on doors until eight a.m. or later, according to their new captain's policy of the police not disturbing anyone between the hours of 9 p.m. and 8 a.m. unless it was an emergency. And a murder investigation, per the new tsar, didn't qualify.

Since she wasn't able to knock on doors, Rebecca found herself searching the streets along with any dumpsters and trash receptacles within a two-block radius. In a trash bin in front of a small corner grocery store, she found a black Coach handbag.

She took it out and opened it. Inside she found a wallet with no credit cards or money, but it did have a driver's license.

"Oh, my God," she murmured. The driver's license photo looked just like the murder victim, but it was the woman's name that most stunned her: Audrey Poole. Auburn hair. Brown eyes. 5'6". 130 lbs. Forty-seven years old. Her driver's license showed the Noriega Street address of Bay-to-Breakers Realty. The same place Rebecca and Sutter had tried to contact the woman with no luck.

Rebecca did find health insurance information, and by contacting them, she obtained Poole's home address. She called Sutter and met him at the address. It was on Vallejo Street, approximately a half-block from the murder scene. It was an older building, but appeared to have been renovated with new, large windows.

Sutter rang the bell for the manager, and they were buzzed inside.

"I can't imagine anyone harming Audrey," Lois Jamieson said after Rebecca and Sutter introduced themselves and explained what had happened. "She was a lovely woman. Doing very well for herself, too."

Rebecca asked to see the victim's apartment, to see if anything there could help catch her killer.

"Oh, of course!"

Jamieson led them to the elevator to the top floor and unlocked Audrey Poole's door. She stood in the doorway as Rebecca and Sutter entered. The apartment was immaculate with a view of San Francisco Bay. It was the sort of place Rebecca could only dream of renting.

"How long did she live here?" Rebecca asked as Bill Sutter headed for the bedroom.

"She bought it a good dozen years ago, I'd say," Jamieson replied.

"Bought it?"

"It's a condominium."

That put a new light on things, Rebecca thought. It also told her Richie probably knew the address and hadn't given it to her. "Did she live alone?" Rebecca asked.

"She did."

As Rebecca looked around, she understood what Richie had been saying about the woman finding a way to make a lot of money. The condo's location and furnishings had to be worth a small fortune.

A den was off the living room and Rebecca entered. The desk was fairly neat, but the room also contained a large filing cabinet. Rebecca opened the cabinet to find it filled with many folders, all listed under a complex numbering system. Rebecca picked up a few folders and flipped through them. Each seemed to pertain to properties sold, but there were many folders for each property. She could only hope this case wouldn't require her to go through all the financial statements and legal documents in this room. If so, she might never finish it.

The desktop was much easier to understand. On it, a small rubber-banded bundle of brochures and business cards showed "Audrey Poole, Realtor" and the business as Bay-to-Breakers Realty. Also, there were several fliers listing homes and apartments for sale throughout the Bay Area. None, however, showed Audrey Poole as the seller's agent. Something seemed a little off here, but nothing jumped out as a cause for murder. And was it only yesterday that Richie had visited the woman?

She knew the news of Poole's murder was going to upset him. He seemed to be genuinely fond of her.

A laptop sat in the middle of the desk, and Rebecca decided the best thing would be to take it back to Homicide and go through it. She also found an iPad, and an older BlackBerry. No smart phone had been in the handbag or anywhere in the apartment that she could see. Yet, she suspected this was a woman who was joined at the hip with her phone. It very likely had been stolen along with the wallet, cash and credit cards.

Soon, Sutter joined her in the den, having found nothing of note elsewhere in the condo.

On the top shelf of a bookcase, Rebecca found an address book. She was surprised it was up there until she opened it and discovered Audrey used it to jot down her passwords. Instead of M being used for friends with last names like Mayfield, for example, it was where she showed "macys.com" followed by a user name and password. Clever. Except too easy to find.

Under A, Rebecca found Apple, plus a four-digit pin, but no phone number.

"Do you have Ms. Poole's cell phone number?" Rebecca asked the manager.

"I do." Mrs. Jamieson hurried off to her place. "I'll be right back with it."

As she waited, Rebecca did a quick perusal of the well-stocked kitchen with a variety of exotic spices. Audrey must have been a good cook. That probably added to her appeal to Richie.

Soon, Lois Jamieson returned. Rebecca called the number she was given, and the BlackBerry rang.

Something wasn't right.

15

R ichie and Vito sat in Richie's favorite booth at the back of the Leaning Tower Taverna on Columbus and Vallejo streets. Richie was digging into a plate of carbonara, and Vito had a meatball sandwich. They always met before Shay arrived since he never ate restaurant food. In fact, Richie almost never saw him eat. Period.

This was the first time he and Vito had eaten together since Richie had been rude to him last Saturday night. Richie still felt bad about that, especially since Vito and Shay had taken it upon themselves to solve his gambler client's debt problem. They convinced him to give away shares of his company stock to the individual he owed as well as to the men who ran the floating game. It was collateral. He either worked hard and bought the stock back, or they could sell his company out from under him. Richie assumed it would work, but at that point, it wasn't his problem. Vito and Shay had done what the client wanted— made his current gambling problem disappear without his wife knowing about it.

Yesterday, Richie had directed the two of them to find out all they could about Audrey Poole's current business dealings, and called this meeting to talk about their findings.

Now, Richie spent most of the meal trying to make up to Vito for his previous foul mood. He claimed he didn't know what had gotten into him.

Well, actually, he did know—Rebecca—but he wasn't about to tell Vito. The problem was between his head and his heart, and Richie was not a person who normally lived a conflicted life. Until lately.

He gave a mournful sigh as he slowly twirled his fork in the pasta, captured some, and stuffed it in his mouth. He washed it down with chianti.

Vito was grateful for Richie's apologies, and ate quietly, occasionally using his finger to stop the spaghetti sauce from escaping the sandwich. He'd look woefully at Richie now and then, but knew better than to try to offer advice where it wasn't wanted.

They were just finishing up when Shay walked in. Richie watched the waitress who had spent the past half hour gushing over him and Vito, give Shay a sullen nod. She knew his cup of hot tea wouldn't result in enough of a tip to warrant a smile.

"Same?" she asked him.

Shay nodded. Her sour expression apparently didn't warrant a spoken response.

"How's it goin'?" Richie asked Shay as he removed his jacket and ascot and slid into the booth beside Vito.

"Not good," Shay said. "Audrey Poole has been murdered."

Vito stopped adding sugar to his coffee, and Richie sat up straight in the seat. He felt as if he'd been sucker-punched. "Murdered? I just saw her yesterday."

"All I can tell you, is I was looking into her financials when the bank moved in and froze everything. I had to back out so my hack wouldn't be found. I checked into why they were doing that and discovered that Poole was dead. They found her on the street not far from her condo. She'd been stabbed."

"Stabbed." Richie shuddered, not able to stop himself from imagining the terror and pain she must have felt. "Damn! Poor kid. She was hiding out, doing all she could to stay safe. This makes me sick. It pisses me off."

"I know she was a friend, boss," Vito said. "I'm sorry."

Richie nodded, trying to pull his emotions together. "Any word yet on who did it?"

"Not that I've heard," Shay said.

"See? Didn't I tell ya?" Vito spoke up. "Something's not right with her business. It ain't natural."

"He's right," Shay said. "And from the little I was able to see, there's more to your ex-client's story, that Steve Burlington, than he's telling you."

"As if another lying client should surprise me." Richie shook his head, Audrey's murder weighing heavily on him. "I don't know why I deal with these scumbags."

"Maybe it's 'cause they're the ones who get into trouble, boss," Vito said. "Like Dante said, pride, envy and avarice are the sparks that set men's hearts on fire. That's why they need you."

Vito's favorite book was Dante's *The Divine Comedy*. After he somehow managed to wade through it in his teens, he decided nothing else was worth reading. He read it again and again, and pulled out quotes at weird times, like now. Richie once swore that if Vito said "Abandon hope, all ye who enter here," one more time, he'd tear his tongue out.

"You had good instincts about this," Richie said finally, ignoring the quote. "I should have listened."

Vito beamed. "It's okay, boss. I think you been distracted."

"Maybe so, but no more." He took a deep breath. "We're going to find whoever killed Audrey and make him pay, dammit. Vito, stick with Bay-to-Breakers Real Estate. With Poole gone, who takes over? Who comes, who goes? Shay, spread out to others in the business. Let's get to the bottom of just what the hell happened to her."

Shay nodded. "Isn't Mayfield on-call this week? If so, Audrey Poole's murder will be her case."

"You even keep track of her schedule now?" Richie asked with a scowl.

"It helps," he replied.

Richie grimaced. "You're right. She's on. Damn, but she's going to be pissed if I start nosing around one of her cases again."

"I know her neighbor was attacked and the woman's assistant killed, but you aren't looking into that without us, are you?" Shay asked.

"Not really. Audrey was the only connection, except that I now know the neighbor, Kiki, was the one screwing up Audrey's latest deal," Richie said.

"And the two deaths, and attack on Kiki, are probably somehow related," Shay said.

"Hard to believe they aren't," Richie said.

"Don'cha think, boss," Vito said, "that you should pay Rebecca a visit and talk about us all working together with her? I mean, we don't wanna step on any toes here, not the Inspector's anyway."

"Pay her a visit, my ass." Richie ran his fingers through his hair, thinking about their last meeting in Homicide. "It'll be like walking on hot coals. But on the other hand, I don't really have a choice."

16

Rebecca requested Audrey Poole's phone and banking records, but they hadn't yet arrived, so she decided to go through the few security tapes she and Sutter had gathered from the area near the crime scene. She hoped she would have more luck with these than she had looking at the street in front of Kiki's spa. Her instincts told her this was more than a robbery gone bad, or a crazed killer stalking lone women. But she needed to rule out those possibilities.

Pacific Heights wasn't the type of neighborhood with much violent crime, which meant its residents were already up in arms about the dead body found in their neighborhood. Even before the victim's name had gotten out, it was clear to them that she might have been one of their own—namely, wealthy. They demanded protection and wanted the city to provide it. Protection from what, no one could say. But the pressure was already mounting on Rebecca and Sutter to clear up this case fast, and to make sure the death happened for a reason, and not because of some random lunatic that might cause general fear and panic.

Rebecca stifled a yawn as she scrolled through the security tapes. Sutter, who hated that kind of desk work, had gone to

Audrey's bank to lean on them to hurry up with the information about Audrey's account. Looking at videos wasn't how homicides were worked in the old days, Sutter liked to say, and he had no intention of working them that new high tech way if he could possibly avoid it. It took shoe leather, he claimed.

It took both, Rebecca believed. But she'd learned long ago not to argue with Sutter. When she did, he sulked, arms folded, and jutted out his lower lip. It was an ugly thing to behold. She preferred to ignore him.

There weren't many security cameras in the area where Audrey had been killed except for the business section of Union Street. To Rebecca's surprise, she spotted Audrey, on foot and alone leaving Pinocchio's Bar and Grill—two doors down from Kiki's place—at 12:45 a.m. At last, a solid lead.

She went to Pinocchio's and asked to speak to everyone who worked there the night before. She showed the staff Audrey Poole's picture. Two people remembered her. One was the bartender who noticed she had entered the bar area alone and sat at a table by herself, but then he lost track of her completely. The other was the cocktail waitress, Lisa Hayes, who served her.

"She's come in here a few times," Hayes said. "Seemed to be a nice lady."

"The bartender seemed to think she was at a table alone. Is that how you remember it?"

"Not exactly." The waitress looked nervous, but that was typical of anyone being interviewed in connection with a murder investigation. "A man came in and joined her."

"Do you know who he was?"

"No."

"Ever see him before?"

"A couple times here, with her."

"What can you tell me about him?" Rebecca asked. "What did he look like?"

"I'm not too sure. It was kind of dark where they sat. I guess he was okay looking, nicely dressed and all. It's usually the guys who are really good-looking that I notice." She couldn't help but smile at that admission. "I think he was probably close to Audrey Poole in age."

Rebecca hated herself for doing it, but she couldn't help asking, "Did he have thick black hair, dark eyes, almost six feet tall, with a slim build? Oh, and a sharp dresser?"

"I don't think he had much hair at all, come to think of it. Or it was really short. And he definitely wasn't slim."

Rebecca let out the breath she'd been holding. She suspected Richie was the type the waitress would remember, but it never hurt to check. "Did they look like they were romantically involved?"

"Um, well, I'm not sure. I mean, the woman—Audrey—paid for their drinks. She got here before him and ordered a dirty martini. Then when he came, she ordered another for herself and the same thing for him. I guess that's okay, but she didn't even ask if that was what he wanted. And then, he left before she did."

"Did he leave a long time before her, or just long enough for her to pay and then meet him outside, perhaps?"

"Um, maybe. But I don't think so. I remember asking if she'd like another drink, but she didn't. So, I guess, she sat there a while."

Rebecca nodded. Richie had told her Audrey was seeing Sean Hinkle. She wished she knew what Sean Hinkle's hair was like these days. She recalled it being on the thin side, maybe thin enough to be scarcely visible in the dark bar. "If you think of anything more, give me a call." She handed Ms. Hayes her card and left the bar.

Rebecca stood a moment out on the sidewalk, the same spot she had seen Audrey on the video tape. She wondered if Audrey had decided to walk home since it wasn't all that far. Unfortunately, she hadn't made it.

Rebecca returned to Homicide. Sutter had received Audrey's home and business landline and BlackBerry cell phone logs, and was now going through them. He found real estate clients and spam, but nothing else. Rebecca doubled-checked his work, and she had to agree. The woman seemed to have no personal life.

But then, Rebecca received an alert on one of Audrey's credit cards. Someone attempted to use it in a liquor store on 6th Street and Folsom, which was near the Hall of Justice.

Rebecca decided it would be easier to walk there than to drive and try to park in that area. Even the illegal spots where cops left their vehicles were usually taken.

The liquor store owner claimed a homeless man had come in trying to use the card. He knew it wouldn't go through, but he played along. When it bounced, he kept it, and now gave it to Rebecca. The homeless guy ran, taking a bottle of Thunderbird with him.

The owner showed Rebecca a picture of the guy on his in-store security camera. He was probably in his fifties, about 5'3", with long gray hair, a beard, and a heavy black jacket that had a strange shine as if from grease. Rebecca thanked the owner and gave him her business card, asking that he call her if the fellow returned.

On her way back to Homicide, turning the corner on 7th Street, she spotted a man sitting in a doorway slugging down some cheap white wine straight from the bottle. Looking at his black pants, dark jacket, long gray hair, and short stature, she walked towards him.

The homeless fellow gawked at her, put the cap on the bottle and then ran. She ran after him.

He turned down an alleyway, then across a traffic-filled

street. Rebecca didn't stop, but kept going. He turned into another alley, but it was a dead-end.

She drew her handgun and held it on him.

"I didn't mean to take the wine!" the man cried. "But I was so thirsty, I couldn't help myself. I'll pay for it." He took some money from his pocket. A fair amount of cash.

"Where did you get all that?" she asked.

He pulled out a five and jammed the rest back in his pocket. "It's mine!"

"If you had cash, why use a credit card at the liquor store?"

"It's going fast. Thought I'd try the card. But the owner got all bent out of shape when it wouldn't go through. I would have paid him, but he started yelling. Here." He held out the money. "Like I said, I'll pay for the wine. I don't want no trouble!" His grimy hand trembled.

"Calm down," she said. "I don't care about your wine."

"No?" His eyes widened in disbelief.

"It's the credit card you tried to use."

"It was my sister's." He quickly shoved the five spot deep into the same pocket as his other bills. "She said I could use it. I tried to tell the store owner."

"And what was your sister's name again?"

"Uh…"

"Right. Where did you get it?"

His brow furrowed.

"Will your memory get any better down at the station?" Rebecca all but yelled the question.

"It was in a garbage can!" He put a hand to his eyes a moment—the other continued to hold his wine tight against his chest—then he added, "Somebody threw it away. I don't know who. I figured I could use it more than sewer rats."

"So you took it," Rebecca said. "What else did you take?"

He reached into another pocket and took out a cell phone. "Here. I can't get it to work anyway."

Audrey's second phone. Of course! She took it. "Anything else?"

He shook his head.

"Any other credit cards?"

He hesitated, looked her in the eyes, then handed over three more.

Rebecca grimaced. Then, although she knew it was a waste of breath, since she used to be a street cop she did her duty. "Don't take wine without paying for it and never try to use cards that aren't yours."

"Yes, ma'am. I'm sorry, ma'am."

"Now get out of here."

Rebecca hurried back to Homicide with the cell phone. She tried some of the 4-digit pins she found scribbled in Audrey Poole's address book, but nothing worked. Apparently, the homeless man's multiple attempts to guess the password resulted in it being locked.

She knew it would be difficult, if not impossible, for her tech staff to break into.

And of course she knew a person who could do it. Shay.

She shook her head. Why was this always happening to her?

She felt bad about the way the conversation had deteriorated when Richie came to give her information about Audrey Poole, and ever since finding Poole dead she had wanted to tell him she was sorry his friend had been murdered. Now, she had a good excuse to call.

Rebecca wasn't sure where the best place would be to meet Richie. She could show up at Big Caesar's, but if she didn't want to stand out in that crowd, she'd have to dress up. She didn't want him to get the wrong impression.

She could ask him to meet her at a bar or restaurant, but that smacked of a date.

She could ask him to come to Homicide, but that was hardly fair. She usually went to the homes of people she needed to talk to, and not drag them into Homicide unless they were suspects or heavily involved in a case.

In short, to treat him the same as anyone else meant going to his house. She expected he would be home around seven o'clock to get ready to go to Big Caesar's for the evening.

She drove to his house near the top of Twin Peaks, an expensive neighborhood of mid-century modern and newer homes near the center of San Francisco. She saw his house lights on. His garage took up the ground floor, and the living area was above it. She parked in the driveway, then walked up the stairs to the front door and knocked.

He looked simultaneously surprised and intrigued to see her. He stiffened his shoulders. "Rebecca, is something wrong? It's not Kiki, is it?"

"Nothing's wrong, and Kiki is doing well, all things considered," she said. "I had hoped to see you earlier. I suspect you've heard about your friend, Audrey."

"Yes." He drew in his breath. "It's hard to believe."

"I wanted to say how sorry I am. I know you liked her."

He waited a moment, then said only, "Thank you."

She found it awkward to be standing in the doorway, yet she understood why he hadn't invited her inside. She drew in her breath. "I've also come by to ask you and Shay for some help."

"About Audrey's murder investigation?" he asked.

"Yes."

"In that case, come inside."

As she walked in, memories of prior visits filled her. She

liked his home. His living room was richly furnished in blues and grays, with a picture window providing a view of the eastern side of San Francisco from the downtown to the bay bridge and the Oakland hills. She stopped a moment, enjoying the view.

"Can I get you something? Wine, coffee maybe?" he asked.

"No thank you. I won't be here long."

He nodded, his lips a firm, straight line, and sat on the sofa.

She took the nearby easy chair, but before she sat, she put a cell phone on the coffee table. "It's Audrey Poole's. I haven't turned it in to the department yet. It's locked, so I know if I give it to them, I'll be ready to retire before they crack into it. I'm hoping you and Shay can get into it and let me see what she was up to."

Richie stared ominously at the device. "Do you have any idea what that could contain? If Audrey was involved with who I think she was involved with, the information in there could be dangerous."

"That's why I'm here."

Richie picked it up and looked it over. "This'll be nothing for Shay. And I want to find out who killed her as much as you do. For me, it's personal."

She nodded. "I know."

He said nothing more, but she found she didn't want to leave. "I'm sorry I treated you badly when you came to Homicide yesterday," she said. "Of course you know what you're doing. I have no business interfering."

"I don't mind hearing your opinion." He rose to his feet.

She took the hint and walked to the door. "Good. Well, goodbye."

"I'll call you when Shay's gotten into the phone." He opened the door for her.

She caught his eye as she stepped out. He looked as if he were about to speak, but then didn't. She understood. There was much she wanted to say as well, but she didn't know how or where to start—or where to end.

He waited a moment.

She turned away, facing the street.

She heard the door softly shut behind her.

17

The next morning at her desk, Rebecca was still fuming about her experience at Richie's house—not at him, but at herself. What was wrong with her? She'd gotten what she wanted. She'd gotten what she wanted. She'd managed to build a barrier between them that made the Great Wall of China pale by comparison. Maybe they could eventually be friends and collaborate from time to time the way he did with Shay and Vito.

An occasional confidential informant, and that's all.

Definitely nothing more.

Why, then, did she feel so miserable?

When she thought about her past relationships, given the way her life was now, they all seemed a bit dull, even boring, and she was glad they hadn't worked out. Someday, she would surely feel the same about Richie.

Although she had to admit, being around him was never boring. She couldn't help but think about Richie and the drug lord, El Grande, not very long ago. That whole episode had scared her to death. She still got the shakes when she thought about how close Richie had come to getting himself killed.

Boring vs. frightening. What a choice.

She needed to find a good man in between the two extremes. Maybe that was the best way, the only way, to get over Richie.

Just then, Homicide's secretary, Elizabeth Havlin, buzzed. Rebecca had a visitor named Luke Barton. She thanked Elizabeth and headed to the office. The only Luke she could think of was Inga's boyfriend, who she had continued to attempt to track down with no luck.

Sitting in the office was a nervous-looking young man wearing jeans and a tee-shirt, a flannel shirt over them as if it were a jacket. He jumped up as soon as he saw her. "I heard you were looking for me."

"You're Inga's friend?"

"Yeah. Well, sort of. I mean, I just met her about a month ago, and we've dated a little. I mean, I'm so sorry to hear she died, I mean, that she was killed and all. I don't know if I can help, but I'm here."

Rebecca took him into the interview room and got his full name and address, and then asked, "Where were you last Saturday night?"

"My old girlfriend moved to Portland. I was up there. We're trying to work it out. We might have, too. I just came back here to pick up my stuff and then I heard the cops were looking for me because of Inga. But I'm moving."

"What's your girlfriend's name?"

He gave her name, address, phone number, and also pulled out a few gas receipts he'd managed to hang onto that showed he drove up last Friday and came back yesterday.

Rebecca made copies of everything, as well as his car registration.

She would check into it, but she suspected his alibi would hold up. She thanked him and sent him on his way.

She was more sure than ever that she was looking for one

solution to the murders of both Audrey Poole and Inga Westergaard, and that Luke Barton had no part in either.

When she returned to her desk, she saw that she had missed a call from FBI special agent, Brandon Seymour.

She couldn't help but wonder if he knew anything about offshore holding companies and investors from China. That seemed right down the FBI's alley. She couldn't help but think of how Seymour was always on the 'right' side of the law, understood and accepted her job as a cop, and had, from the time they first worked together, made it quite clear he would like to go out with her. Any time, any place.

Seemed like a no brainer.

She picked up the phone and punched in his number.

Rebecca spent the rest of the afternoon going through Inga Westergaard's family, friends, and business connections, and ended up with nothing that caused her cop instincts to light up. She then switched to putting together pieces of Audrey Poole's life and business, and contacting Poole's most recent US-based business clients. She quickly found they were among the most closed-mouth people she'd ever met. She got nowhere with any of them.

She next turned to Audrey's bank records about her holding company. One look at the complex transactions and foreign bank involvement told her it would take someone with a lot more knowledge of business than she had, like a forensic auditor.

She gritted her teeth as, once again, the fact that Shay claimed to have an MBA from the Wharton School of Business wasn't lost on her. She was *not* going to go asking Richie for any more favors.

She came across the name of Audrey's accountant, Bridget McMillan. Good. Who needed Shay, anyway?

She tried calling the accountant, and like everyone else she needed to reach in this case, the call went to messaging. She left a message, and then several more as time passed and she received no call back.

Ironically, the more she looked into both Inga and Audrey's lives, and investigated their murders, the *less* sense it made for their deaths to be connected.

Finally, she gave up wrestling with these cases and left work to go to the hospital to visit Kiki. She found Kiki asleep and still lightly sedated from her surgery, so Rebecca didn't disturb her. She spent a little time with Sierra who hadn't left her mother's side and then continued on her way home.

After left-over pizza and a salad for dinner, she went upstairs to visit her landlord.

Bradley Frick was still a nervous wreck about the break-in and the murder of Kiki's assistant. He was about Rebecca's height, fairly bony, with bleached blond hair that he wore in a spiked style, despite being too old for it. He was somewhere in his forties, although he dressed and acted as if he were still in his twenties. Or younger. He made his fortune as a software developer by selling his product to Google. He tried to explain to Rebecca what it did, but she never understood anything beyond it being some sort of algorithm to track purchasing power.

Rebecca tried to calm him down, but at the moment, he was sure that Tierra del Fuego, the southernmost tip of South America, was the place to be.

Finally, unable to take his nervous paranoia a moment longer, she went back to her apartment.

It was funny, but as she opened the door, she could all but see Richie on the sofa, Spike on his lap, a beer at his side, and ESPN on the TV.

But the sofa was empty and the TV off. Spike looked happy to see her, but even he seemed to recognize something, or someone, was missing.

She found an old movie she loved, *Ghost,* a romantic fantasy. She had to chuckle as she thought of how much Richie would despise a maudlin movie like that. She had a good cry over it, then went to bed.

18

Richie sat at a table at the St. Francis Hotel's Clock Bar, watching the entrance. Finally, about fifteen minutes late, his ex-client, Steve Burlington, strolled in. Being kept waiting had put Richie, who was already not thrilled with the world, in a crummy mood.

"Why here?" Richie said as Burlington joined him. "I didn't know you like fancy joints like this."

"I like it when I don't want to run into anyone I know." Burlington's tone was harsh. "Here, we can talk."

A waiter came by and Burlington ordered a cosmopolitan. Richie already had a craft-brewed IPA in front of him.

"Okay," Richie said, staring hard at Burlington. "Talk."

Burlington grimaced. "I'm sure you know Audrey Poole has been murdered."

"I know," Richie said.

Burlington pushed back a little way from the table. "It's a damned shame. Poor Audrey. But the timing really sucks! Goddamn it, Richie. I don't know what I'm going to do."

Richie's eyes narrowed. "What do you mean?"

The waitress brought his drink and Burlington took a long

sip. "Crap!" He rubbed his temples a moment. "Her buyers still want that property, wouldn't you say?"

"I have no idea."

"The fact that she's dead shouldn't change that," Burlington sounded as if he was trying to convince himself more than Richie.

"I thought you don't know who the buyers are, right?" Richie asked. "The way I understand it, the deal would have gone through Poole, and those offshore holding companies are set up so that the buyers' identities are kept secret. All legal documents are in the possession of the trust and its accountant. With Audrey Poole gone, you don't know who is going to finish setting up the sale for the trust."

"She should have had a partner, dammit, someone to work with in case something like this happened!"

Richie was disgusted. "I doubt finding someone to finish her case work if she was ever murdered was high on her list of priorities."

"A deal's a deal," Burlington said fiercely. "I'm not going to get a better deal than the one we worked out. All I need is to find out who wants my building and then I can negotiate directly with the buyers."

"Take it easy," Richie said.

"I need your help," Burlington said.

"I don't deal with this stuff."

"I'm talking a ten million dollar price tag! Audrey Poole would have gotten a ten percent commission. I'll pay you what I would have paid her if you make this happen. You've been involved in real estate before. You can do it."

Richie had to take a moment, more than one in fact, to digest what he'd just heard.

"A million dollars? Are you kidding me?"

"I'm serious as a heart attack."

Richie hated that expression. Leave it to Burlington to use it. "Okay. Let me look into it. Right now, I have no idea if it'll be possible. We'll need to wait and see who takes over Bay-to-Breakers and the deals Audrey had going, if anyone. In the meantime, don't go spending your money, or even making obligations for it, until we get this sorted out. You hear me?"

"But that's the problem, damn it! I've got debts. People to pay."

"They're going to have to wait."

"They won't. You've got to help me, Richie. This isn't my fault. But the guys I owe money to won't see it that way. I made a commitment and they'll expect me to meet it."

Richie shook his head. Burlington had money, a lot of money. He had no business getting himself in such a bind. But for the possibility of making a million dollars, Richie would certainly try to sort everything out for him. "I'll see what I can do."

His phone rang. It was Shay with news about his findings on Audrey Poole's phone.

And Shay was just the person he needed to talk to.

Richie knew he'd have to contact Rebecca soon about the contents of Audrey's phone. But he also knew there was one major contact that Rebecca and the entire SFPD would have little success talking to.

He headed for Chinatown.

Richie had grown up on the edge of Chinatown, so while many of his friends were of Italian descent from North Beach, a large number were Chinese. He'd spent nearly as much time in Chinatown as he had in the Italian and "American" parts of the city and was equally fascinated with the history of the area.

He also learned a lot about hard work, making money, and familial loyalty from his Chinese friends. Now, he turned into Ross Alley and parked. It didn't look like anything much, but it had once been a favorite spot for the so-called "hatchet men" of San Francisco lore to hold their tong wars. Opposing tongs would line the walls of the alley facing each other. Then, all at once, both sets of fighters would run together wielding hatchets, knives, and sometimes guns. The battle would continue for only a matter of minutes and end as quickly as it began. Bodies— dead, mutilated, or merely maimed—covered an alley awash in blood as those fighters still able to move fled the scene.

Now, the headquarters of Chinatown's influential Five Family Association was situated in one of the old brick-covered buildings in the alley. Richie knew that the word "tong" meant "association," and in Chinese had no negative connotation. Also, the old-style fighting tongs had been wiped out of the city in the 1920's.

Beginning in the 1970's, however, a new kind of gang had moved into the area, creating a sinister underworld beneath the strings of red paper lanterns, restaurants, joss temples, and narrow alleyways that attracted tourists to the nation's oldest Chinatown. As a new flood of immigrants from Hong Kong and mainland China moved into the city, many of them knew no English, and had no knowledge of how to make their way in the new culture in which they found themselves. They were drawn to methods used for centuries in their homeland, which meant going to an "association" to seek safety, money, and other aid.

Soon, several of these "associations" devolved into secret societies known as triads. Their goal was to obtain money and power by whatever means possible. Once they had that money and power, they would do whatever it took to keep it, which mostly involved fighting with other triads.

Growing up, Richie had heard a lot about the Wah Ching,

Hop Sing, and Joe's Boys triads. The most well-known incident, a shootout in a restaurant filled with tourists, happened in 1977. But there had been other much less known gunfights in which no tourists were involved. Chinese were, however. Eventually, the Wah Ching moved to Los Angeles, and the Wo Hop To gained power in the city. The Jackson Street Boyz, which included Vietnamese immigrants, were at the top of the power structure at the moment. The whole thing was something Richie knew better than to mess with. Triad members not only dealt with street crimes like stealing cars or drug-dealing, but also sophisticated money-making schemes such as credit-card fraud, racketeering, illegal gambling.

He couldn't help but wonder if the kind of deals Audrey was involved in hadn't also caught their interest. The tentacles of these triads had spread throughout California, including politics. When an FBI sting caught a state senator with ties to Chinatown a few years back for accepting money and campaign donations in exchange for providing official favors as well as helping broker an arms deal, it cast a harsh light on Chinatown's tight-knit network of tongs and triads.

That was why, when Shay found a number of phone calls between Audrey Poole and the head of the Five Families Association, Richie became immediately worried about Rebecca. It was a hornet's nest she didn't want to overturn.

He went into the association building and asked to speak to Milton Jang.

Richie was quickly shown into Jang's office. He had been there before, but the lavish decor still took his breath away. It was filled with beautiful antique Chinese vases, porcelains, and paintings from long ago dynasties. The furniture Jang used, however, had been hand carved in San Francisco as a means of continuing the creative tradition in younger generations. The gold that adorned many pieces, Richie had been told, stemmed from the days of the Forty-Niner California gold rush, which first brought thousands of Chinese men to "Gold Mountain" to seek their fortunes.

Jang put down his cigarette and then stood with his hand outstretched. "It's been a long time, Richie."

Richie clasped it. "Too long, my friend."

Jang smiled broadly as the two shook hands. He was a withered little man who dyed his hair to keep it jet black instead of gray, and who enjoyed Armani suits and silk shirts. His teeth were stained grayish yellow and black rimmed from too many harsh, filterless cigarettes from the Chinese mainland. And, Richie figured, a culture that not long ago believed that women blackening their teeth was a sign of beauty, probably saw nothing wrong with Jang's mouth. "Have a seat. Tell me what brings you here when you should be out with that lovely homicide detective I hear you are seeing."

Richie grinned. "It seems your spies are as busy as always."

"They have to work hard to keep up with yours," Jang said eying him sharply.

A young woman came in with a tray of hot tea and Chinese-style almond cookies. Her teeth, Richie noticed at the same time as he noticed how drop-dead gorgeous she was, were sparkling white.

He gladly took the tea, passing on the cookies she offered.

Soon, she bowed and left the room. Jang cocked his head slightly as if waiting to hear what Richie had to say.

As Jang finished his cigarette, Richie told him about the Union Street building that Audrey Poole wanted to sell, and the overseas Chinese buyers she had lined up. He explained that the building's tenant had a lease she refused to give up, but she had been badly beaten and her employee murdered. And now, Audrey Poole had been stabbed to death.

"Audrey Poole said she had no idea who was behind the

purchase she wanted to make," Richie added. "She said it was all done electronically, and that her buyers were in China. I'm wondering if you know anything about this kind of set up."

Jang sipped his tea and didn't speak for a long time as he pondered Richie's story. Soon, he took out a pack of cigarettes covered with Chinese writing and offered Richie one. Richie quickly shook his head. He'd given up the habit years ago. Usually, the smell of a cigarette under his nose still tempted him. Not this time. The scent was somewhere between dung and heap.

Jang smirked at him and put one between his lips and lit it. "Audrey Poole lied to you."

"Did she?" Richie asked.

"She worked with someone right here in this city. You know him as Timothy Yan, but we call him Yan Jing Sheh which means 'The Cobra' because he strikes as fast and is as deadly. He was a lieutenant for 'Shrimp Boy,' but now that 'Shrimp Boy' is back in prison, Yan is on his own. Unfortunately, he is every bit as dangerous. Stay out of his way. If he wants someone's property, they should think a long time before saying no. Do you know why he wants the property?"

Richie didn't like hearing any of this. Stephen Chow, known as "Shrimp Boy" because that was his grandmother's pet name for him due to his small stature, was a tong member involved in the infamous 1977 restaurant massacre. After surviving that, he became head of the Wo Hop To Triad. Shrimp Boy might be in prison, but anyone associated with him, like this "Cobra," was no one to mess with.

"I understand Audrey Poole's buyers want two parcels on Union," Richie said. "The plan was to tear both down and build apartments."

Jang nodded. "Ah, in that case, they plan to make much money. People in China are becoming wealthy, but they know the country can change its laws in an instant. Because of that, rich Chinese will pay a lot of money to have a child born in America. I suspect the apartments will be for wealthy wives to live in comfort while they await the birth of their new US citizens. Once the child is born here, everything changes as far as the family members being allowed to enter and stay in this country. More and more people want to have children with this dual-citizenship. It may be a matter of life or death, wealth or poverty, for an entire family in the future. People are willing to pay a lot for such security."

"Fascinating," Richie said. "So one spa owner tried to stand in the way of all that."

"You say, she survived?" Jang asked, one eyebrow cocked.

"Yes."

"She's very lucky. Or, she was not a victim of the Cobra. If she was, she wouldn't still be breathing."

Richie feared that was true.

"Also," Jang continued, "these people don't care who gets in their way, including the police."

Richie's eyes narrowed. "What are you saying?"

"If your friend gets caught up in these real estate dealings while trying to find a murderer, it could be very bad for her. Right now, I don't believe the Cobra or his people are involved in any of this, but tomorrow, who knows? You should talk to her, convince her to drop this line of pursuit. Perhaps, if she's willing to look the other way, maybe for some money ..."

"No way."

Jang heaved a sigh. "I'm afraid, my friend, if she digs too far and makes people nervous, her fortune will not be a happy one."

Richie's jaw clamped tight, then he gave a slight nod of the head. "I understand."

Hinkle's phone vibrated. He had received a text message. He opened it.

—*That nightclub owner is talking to important people in Chinatown. This will not be tolerated. You must act. Now!*

Hinkle dropped to his knees. He knew the consequence if he didn't act.

Rebecca was glad to leave Homicide at six p.m., rush home to change clothes, and to make herself look good for a Friday night date. Well, not exactly a date ... but close.

Brandon Seymour would be picking her up at seven-thirty. He had called with a simple question about SFPD procedures, which he could have easily found an answer to anywhere. She asked him about foreign money coming into the country via real estate deals. He suggested dinner to discuss the complex subject properly.

She agreed.

She even decided to wear a dress, a form-fitting dress in rose pink with modest elbow-length sleeves offset by a rather daring V-neck bodice.

She had unlocked the door to the breezeway and told him to go through it to her front door and knock.

When she opened the door, and he looked at her, his eyebrows rose and a pleased smile covered his face. "Hello."

That was the reaction she'd hoped for as she decided to wear a dress and high heels. She had to admit that he looked quite nice in a light blue sweater that matched the color of his eyes over a blue-and-white striped shirt and gray dress slacks. With his short-clipped blond hair and stern, muscular build, he could have been a prototypical model for a "G-man."

She grabbed her coat and handbag and they walked the couple of blocks to a German restaurant.

As Rebecca eyed a number of intriguing appetizers on the menu, foods she'd never had but was willing to try, Brandon said, "I don't think we need to bother with appetizers. Their entrees are huge."

She ordered sauerbraten with spätzle and a "pancake soup," and, to her surprise, Brandon chose a steak.

"No German food?" she asked.

"I don't care for spicy food," he said.

Spicy? German? "You should have said so before we came here," she said.

"It's okay. As long as a place serves steak or burgers, I'm fine."

"Great," she murmured, then smiled.

The conversation quickly turned to off-shore holding companies. Brandon knew a lot about them, including oversight by a Federal agency she had never heard of, the Financial Crimes Enforcement Network section of the Treasury. He gave her a lot of details about how they're set up. She tried to keep her mind focused on what he was saying, but he did have a tendency to drone.

She kept a smile on her face, however. He was a pleasant fellow in a stiff and polished way, and extremely thoughtful. A good date—if this were a date, which it was not.

She realized her smile was sagging woefully as he prattled about legal ramifications of international banking laws on offshore holding companies.

She gulped down some beer. He didn't know much about wines, which was fine. Neither did she. He had ordered a Miller Lite to go with his steak. She asked the waitress for a German beer, and had been given a hoppy ale. As she watched him eat, she realized it was probably a good thing he didn't know wines since he ate the steak and downed his beer so quickly she didn't see how he even knew what he was ingesting. He had, rather annoyingly, finished his meal before she was even half-way through hers. The waitress then cleared his dishes, making her feel as if she were holding up progress.

"Enough about all that," he said.

She jarred herself back. "Yes. It's all interesting."

"I can't tell you how nice it is to go out with someone like you who understands and appreciates the work I do."

"Of course, I do. I admire it."

"It's great to hear, Rebecca. You know, I was married once. My wife didn't understand ..."

She tuned out again. Nothing like the old "my wife didn't understand my job, and it destroyed my marriage" routine—the bane of too many in law enforcement. *Tell me a new one, Brandon.*

But he didn't. Eventually, he asked if she'd like some dessert.

"No, thanks. I'm fine," she said. *Let me out of here!*

"How about we try a sports bar? There are plenty around. Or, if you like to dance, we can take in a night spot with live music."

"I'm so sorry, I don't think so. I should head back home."

He looked disappointed, but paid the bill and they quickly walked up the hills to her building in Mulford Alley.

As he stood on the sidewalk, she unlocked the door to the breezeway. He put his hand on it as if to give it a push as soon as she turned the knob, clearly expecting to walk inside with her.

She faced him. "I'd invite you in, but I'm on-call tonight," she said, forcing that same big smile once again. "I should try to get a little sleep before the late night calls start to come in. That's when most murders happen in this city, as I'm sure you know."

"On call? I didn't realize that," he said.

"Yes. It happens quite often," she said, still smiling.

He grinned. "I'm very good at warming a cup of milk. It helps a person sleep, you know. So does a little neck and shoulder massage." He held up his hands. "These hands can work magic. Trust me."

She laughed. "I'm sure they can. But not tonight."

His smile vanished and a flash of irritation filled his face.

"Thank you for the lovely meal," she said quickly. "I had a nice time."

His countenance relaxed as he took her hand. "Me, too. Maybe we can do this again?"

"I hope so," she said.

He leaned forward and gave her a kiss. She didn't stop him, but she did nothing to deepen the kiss or to encourage him. He stepped back as if knowing her heart wasn't in it. "I'll call," he promised.

"Thanks. Good night." With that, she entered the breezeway, shut the door behind her, and then took a deep breath of relief. But as she walked along the breezeway, working her jaw because it actually had begun to ache from all that smiling, she was suddenly struck with guilt that she hadn't been nicer to him. Logically, there was nothing wrong with the man. He might have been excruciatingly boring simply because it was their first date, or "almost" date, and he was nervous. Maybe she should go out with him again. To give him another chance and all.

Was she being unfair?

She stepped past the breezeway into the yard and froze.

Richie sat on the bench by the planter box playing catch with Spike. He wore a heavy black turtleneck sweater and black slacks. For some reason, she always found a black turtleneck on a man wonderfully sexy. "Where's your friend?" he asked with a smile and a too jolly tone to his voice.

Her initial reaction was joy at seeing him, but his smile

squashed that. And then she had to wonder why he was there. He had a cup of coffee at his side—she recognized the cup from her apartment. Nothing like making yourself at home, Amalfi, she thought. In fact, the more she thought about it, the more irritated she grew, as if all the smiles and niceness she had forced upon herself while with Seymour, had drained her of any further good will. "What in the hell are you doing here?"

His infuriating smile grew broader. A lot broader. "I'm glad to see you didn't invite him in. That would have been awkward."

"Only for you when I threw you out!" she shouted. "If you're through spying on me, you can leave now."

Her apartment door was wide open, so she stormed inside, took hold of the door and spun around to slam it, when Spike trotted forward to enter the apartment with Richie right behind him.

"You look nice," he said softly as he took the door from her and shut it. "Real nice." His gaze drifted over her dress and high heels. He seemed to swallow hard.

So did she. Something in his gaze made her feel warm inside. "I don't always wear jeans, you know." She tried to keep an angry tone. It wasn't working.

"I know." He stepped towards her.

Her breathing quickened, and she stepped back. "Aren't you supposed to be working tonight?"

"They can manage without me."

She tossed the handbag and coat she'd been carrying onto the sofa. "I won't even ask how you knew I went to dinner with Bran—to talk about my case, by the way—but since you did, why put yourself in the position of being here if I invited him in?"

"Bran, is it? How chummy. And I'm sure his interest was totally about your murder investigation." His mouth tightened, and he marched into the kitchen. "Want some coffee? I'm here because I've got news about the case." His voice was curt and hard now. "And that would be true even if that muscular bobble head-looking FBI honcho had come in here with you."

And then he added, "Of course, seeing me here, he might not have stayed ..."

So he did care that she went out with Brandon. For some reason, she found the thought exceedingly pleasing. "No thanks on the coffee. What's your news?"

He took from his pocket what she immediately recognized as Audrey Poole's cell phone. He then sat beside her, turned the phone on and showed her some most interesting findings. "The first thing you need to know is the phone was under Audrey's mother's name, Cynthia Poole. Audrey apparently also used her deceased mother's credit card to pay for it. That's why you couldn't find anything connected with this phone."

Rebecca nodded. "Clever."

He continued. "There are a number of calls between Audrey Poole and Sean Hinkle. She told me they were in bed together more because of business than love, and I mean that literally. Particularly the past two weeks, Audrey and Hinkle spoke daily, sometimes more than once a day. The last day of her life, a number of phone calls passed between them, including one at eleven, a couple of hours before her death."

"Eleven?" That was enough time for them to arrange to meet at Pinocchio's on Union a little before midnight. Rebecca now had a good idea who Audrey might have met with the night she was killed.

"Shay told me that the details of her offshore holding company are kept on an overseas private server in the Bahamas, and she would log into it from the phone. Just about everything was done on it, particularly setting up her real estate deals." He stood, handed her the phone and then moved to the rocking chair facing the sofa, as if he was uncomfortable sitting so close to her. She had to admit, she found his nearness a definite distraction.

He quickly added, "Audrey also had a number of calls from my friend, the building inspector."

She tried to pay attention to what he was saying. "Your friend?"

"Not really. He's a big, balding fellow who I suspect helped her find distressed property to sell, although she denied it when I asked. Still, a lie or two meant nothing to Audrey."

She was finding this tale confusing. "Audrey lied to you?"

"She lied."

"I see," Rebecca said, trying to put this together with the details she had learned from Brandon. "So your pal the building inspector found places for Audrey to buy for less than they were worth."

"Exactly. From what I've seen, if he found a house that fit what Audrey wanted, the fix was in," Richie said. "He would give the owner some bad news, the owner would then call Audrey for help, and, like magic, she'd come up with foreign investors for a prime piece of real estate at a distressed property price."

"Are you sure?"

He shook his head. "I have no proof, if that's what you're asking. But it makes sense, especially in light of the reaction of the building inspector to my attempt to bribe him."

Did she hear that right? "You tried to bribe a building inspector?"

"Of course. I've been fairly lucky getting 'extras' from people in city government for a few bucks. Not all, by any means, but let's just say quite a bit of business is done under the table. I tried that, and the inspector said he wasn't interested. He wouldn't consider doing anything with the property other than suggesting the owner have Audrey sell it. That tells me a lot."

She just shook her head. She wondered if she'd ever 'get'

these people the way Richie did. She had been scrolling through the list of personal contacts as they talked, but now she stopped. "There are so many names here."

"She was in business a long time," Richie offered. "Let me show you something else Shay came up with." He opened up a spread sheet. It showed a great number of high payments going into an offshore bank account, and also a lot of payments leaving it. "Shay found payments from the holding company going to one name in Audrey's contacts that isn't an investor. The name is Sean Hinkle." Richie continued.

"Sean," she murmured. "Again, the city government connection."

"Which means a lot of people you probably don't want to upset," Richie said. "Especially since you work for them."

"I'll go wherever this investigation takes me."

"That's what I'm afraid of," Richie muttered. "So tell me, who is your prime suspect?"

"You know I can't discuss an on-going investigation."

"Motive?"

She shook her head.

"What can you tell me?"

Her shoulders sagged. "Only that we're going in circles, and nothing makes sense."

"Earlier today, I met with one of the most influential people on Audrey's phone contacts, one she's exchanged a number of calls with. Milton Jang, head of the Five Families Association in Chinatown. He knew a lot about Audrey's business. More than she had admitted to, in fact."

He explained everything to her, from Audrey's offshore holding company, to the involvement of Yan Jian Sheh, aka Timothy Yan, aka "The Cobra," in wanting to purchase the building with Kiki's spa.

She frowned. She'd already run into several Chinese names

in this investigation, and they were still pretty much a mystery to her. "Okay, so this Cobra apparently wants the building with Kiki's spa," she said. "So, by attacking her and Inga, especially if he killed them both, the spa would be closed and Audrey could make the sale, and the Cobra would be happy, right?"

"Right."

"So, why would he kill Audrey?" she asked.

He thought a moment. "Maybe because she was the only one who could point to him as the killer. Or, I should say, his men. Guys like the Cobra never do their own wet work."

"Wet work? That sounds like something Shay might say."

"Except it's true. Audrey said she had an idea who might be behind all this, but she was scared to name him. With the Cobra, that would make sense. I'd be too scared to name him, too, frankly."

"That's awful," Rebecca murmured.

"I want to help you find whoever killed her, Rebecca." His words were firm and harsh.

"I know you do, and we'll find him—or her. We won't give up," Rebecca said.

"Audrey wasn't a bad person," he said. "And she didn't deserve to die this way."

Rebecca studied him a moment, then nodded. "The hardest part of my job is to face friends and families of victims because so often they're exactly that—good, innocent people, trying to get along and make a go of it in a tough world, and they pay the ultimate price. That's also why I care about my job. If I do it right, I can get some justice for those victims. I know it's not much in the end, but it's better than them being forgotten."

His gaze met and studied hers a long while. "I have to agree with you," he murmured. "Still, you can't forget that Audrey was involved with big money players, and they know you're involved in the search for her killer. Milton Jang is a friend, somewhat, and he tried to warn me. He doesn't think the Cobra, or any triad, was involved in Audrey's murder, but they could well be involved in her business. If you dig too close to them, things will become very dangerous for you."

"I hear you," she said. "I don't really believe I'm in any danger at this time." She sighed. "But now, I've got to get some sleep. I'm on-call tonight."

He walked to the door. "No, you're not. Was that the excuse you used to give Brandon Seymour the heave-ho tonight?"

She studied him a long moment. "You'll never know, will you?"

He rolled his eyes and faced the door, but then turned back, put his hands on her shoulders, pulled her close, and as he wrapped his arms around her, he gave her a kiss that could have set her hair on fire. She didn't want to think that she kissed him back, but she probably did. Probably, definitely did.

All she knew for sure was that she could scarcely catch her breath as he let her go and left the apartment.

Poor Brandon, she thought, as she contemplated the difference between the two goodnight kisses. He didn't stand a chance.

21

Bridget McMillan stuffed a bunch of clothes into her suitcase and put them in her car. She should have left as soon as she heard Audrey Poole had been murdered, but she'd wanted to finish a couple of accounts first. *Stupid, stupid!* But she took pride in her work. She'd been an accountant for over thirty years, and she was a darn good one.

And Audrey Poole's Bay-to-Breakers Realty was her top client. Bridget had never before known anyone who'd been murdered. Even living in a big city where crime was fairly common compared to her hometown, Laramie, Wyoming, she still hadn't known anyone violently killed, or even assaulted. Not a single robbery or burglary, in fact. Until now.

At least, she told herself, no one should care what she was doing with "B2B," which was how she showed the company's name in her books, or that she might know much at all about the offshore holding company. And no one should care that she had access to the names connected to the accounts, should they? Of course not. Nothing to worry about.

She took a few deep breaths to calm herself as she finished packing her car and put a bag of Funions, a box of Ding Dongs, and a package of Pecan Sandies on the passenger seat in case she got hungry as she drove. Plus a sixteen-ounce bottle of diet Pepsi. Ms. Poole's death was a random robbery attempt, she told herself, not anyone wanting to murder her because of who, or what, she was. This was so because it had to be.

But Bridget couldn't be sure of that, and some of the people Audrey had worked with were well-known, too well-known. And some were dangerous.

Bridget was heading up the coast to the small house she'd bought a few years back, a vacation get-away just for her. She'd stay there until the police caught Audrey's killer. A week or two should do it, she hoped. The house was on a half-acre, near the town of Jenner.

She told her friend Dory where she was going, but other than that, no one particularly knew or cared what she did. She pretended she liked her life that way, pretended she didn't, at times, ache with loneliness. But other times, such as now, it wasn't a lie at all. She wanted nothing so much as to hide.

At seven o'clock, she got into her car and headed north. It would be dark before she reached the Sonoma coast and Jenner, but she knew the road well. It didn't scare her.

Truth be told, the scariest part of the drive was along Highway 1, the Pacific Coast Highway, which was filled with treacherous sharp curves along the sides of cliffs that, if missed, would result in a deadly drop to the rocks and water far below. She was always careful driving that highway, despite the people who would tailgate and give her the finger for her cautious speed. Better safe than sorry was her motto.

She soon saw the Golden Gate Bridge in her rear-view mirror. Being no fool, she stayed on the multi-laned Highway 101 as long as she could, but at Petaluma, she had to turn westward towards the ocean. By nine o'clock she had reached Highway 1. This part of the road, this part of the state, was quite empty. A couple of cars came up behind her, and as soon as she found a space to move over, she did, or they took a chance on one of the infrequent straight stretches of road to pass her. She hated people passing, but she hated speeding even more.

She was past Bodega Bay and going along a patch of highway edging the ocean when a large truck pulled up behind her. It came so close she could make out its Dodge logo. She slowed down a bit, hoping the driver would pass. Instead, he slowed down and came even closer. She would have pulled over except there was no room. The ocean was on her left, and a hillside on her right. She tried speeding up, but the truck stayed with her.

All right, she thought. If he was going to be that way, she'd slow down until he was forced to pass.

The truck hit her back bumper. She jolted forward as fear coursed through her. Was he crazy?

She sped up again, hoping to find a space to pull over, another road, a driveway, anything, to get away from the madman.

The road curved, and she could feel her little Nissan Versa trying to hug the pavement as she went into the turn far too rapidly. It was a great car for city driving, for those times when she didn't simply take the bus. It was especially great for squeezing into tiny parking spaces so she didn't have to spend $20 for a half-hour to park in a lot. But at the moment, she wished she were driving a tank.

The back of the car skidded from side-to-side, scaring her. She automatically put on the brakes, only to find the truck right behind her again.

She kept going, driving fast when the road straightened, and slowing down before hitting a curve. No one else was anywhere out here. She would have tried to call for help, except that she knew from experience there was no cell service in this area.

She might have tried to flag down a passing driver, except that she couldn't imagine anyone stopping for her. And besides, there were no passing drivers.

Perspiration beaded on her forehead. She didn't know if her car had begun to shake, or if she was doing it.

The truck hit her again.

What's wrong with him?

She felt tears come to her eyes. Tears of fright and frustration. There were no street lights out here. Nothing except the small headlights of her car, and the enormous beams from the truck that filled her car and bounced off her rear-view mirror, all but blinding her. Fear tried to paralyze her, but she fought it. She kept her gaze glued to the white line between the lanes, though at times, she drifted way over it when taking a curve.

Why is he doing this to me?

The truck hit her again, much harder this time, causing her neck to snap forward and back. The thought flashed momentarily that some damage might have been done; that she would have to go to the doctor and probably wear a neck brace. But that thought immediately vanished for one much more pressing.

The truck all but latched onto her rear bumper and was now pushing her. She tried to steer around a curve. She turned, but only a little. And her car no longer gripped the road.

Soon, she felt nothing beneath her tires but air.

22

Rebecca spent Saturday and Sunday with Kiki's children. Kiki's doctors reported that there was no longer any fluid leakage, and the brain swelling was receding. Kiki wasn't out of the woods yet, but everyone was hopeful.

Rebecca didn't hear anything more from Brandon or Richie, so it turned out that the only male she met with all weekend for a little food and wine was her landlord, Bradley Frick.

At times, life was the pits.

First thing Monday morning, Rebecca headed for City Hall. Although it was still located on Van Ness Avenue, in the same place as always, a few years ago the good superintendents of the city decided to change the street name of its location to "Dr. Carlton B. Goodlett Place," named after a medical doctor, civil rights leader, newspaper publisher, and local political force. That simple change caused an untold amount of confusion to newcomers to the city, and even, for a while, the US Post Office.

Rebecca always enjoyed entering City Hall. Its rotunda was large and lavish, and its dome even higher than the US Capitol Building. It was completed in 1913 after the original city hall—a much larger and allegedly even more beautiful building—was destroyed in the city's 1906 earthquake.

She went up to the second floor which housed the mayor's chambers in a series of rooms. Rebecca first entered a large main reception area filled with security. She showed her credentials and asked to speak to Sean Hinkle. He was contacted, and she was directed down a hall of mayoral portraits to the staff offices.

Sean Hinkle met her in a small reception area. The first thing she looked at was his hair and discovered he had a lot less than she remembered. He was what was often referred to as "prematurely balding," with a short fringe of brown hair above his ears and the back of his head, and a few longer strands like lonely wanderers across the top of his head. He had also grown a bit portly. He looked nervous, but almost immediately flashed a smile.

"Rebecca, how nice to see you," he said. "You're looking great. And congratulations on becoming a homicide detective. I know you always wanted that position."

"Thank you, Sean," she said. "I'm enjoying the job a lot. And I hope you're enjoying working for the mayor."

"Well, you know, I always felt I could pick a winning team." He beamed. He was a pleasant looking man, not exceptional by any means, but she remembered why she had gone with him on a few dates. "And obviously, this time I was right. But enough of all this. I'm assuming you're here on business."

"I am. Can we take this to a more private location?"

"Given your position, that's actually rather unnerving," he admitted wryly. "Since the mayor is out of the office today, let's go to his lounge."

He took her arm and walked her through the mayor's official office, an impressive, high-ceilinged, wood-paneled room. Behind it was a small hallway and kitchen area. He offered coffee or a soft drink. She refused.

They continued down the hall. "Have you been here before?" he asked.

"Never," she said.

"You've got to see this, then." He showed her an all marble bathroom.

"Oh, wow."

"It's the mayor's john," he said with a chuckle. She smiled. They continued on.

"And here's something else you don't want to miss." His demeanor completely changed as he gently opened the door to a surprisingly small room. In a somber, hushed voice he said, "This is now a storage area, but it had been Mayor George Moscone's personal office." Moscone had been mayor in the 1970's and was murdered in that very spot by one of the city's supervisors. The supervisor, whose infamous defense was that he ate too many Twinkies, had also killed fellow supervisor Harvey Milk. She could understand why the tragic space had been turned into a store room.

At the end of the hall they reached the lounge. It was a sports-themed room filled with photos and memorabilia mostly from the city's great Giants and 49er teams.

Hinkle took a seat on a leather sofa, and Rebecca sat on an adjacent matching leather loveseat. She began her questioning immediately. "I suspect you're aware that an acquaintance of yours, perhaps more than an acquaintance, Audrey Poole, was recently found murdered."

He dropped his gaze and nodded. "I read about that." His voice was soft. "Absolutely horrible! She was a good person, a fun person."

"I'm talking to people who knew her," Rebecca explained, "trying to find any leads as to why someone wanted her dead. I'd like to ask you a few questions."

"Well, sure. I don't know that I can help, but I'll try."

"Thank you. We're still working on a motive. Can you tell me what your involvement was with her or her business?"

He looked uncomfortable. "We dated a few times. That's all."

"Recently?"

He grinned. "Are you asking if I'm free again?"

She didn't return the smile, but waited for a serious answer.

"Sorry." He looked embarrassed. "I'm a master at bad timing. And bad jokes. We dated, but I think both of us realized that it wasn't really working out."

"Looking at her phone records, the two of you were in contact on an almost daily basis."

"Her phone records? I don't—"

"We found her personal phone. The one listed under a different name."

"Whatever," he said dismissively. "We were friends. We talked a lot. That's it."

"I'm interested in her business dealings. I understand many were with foreign investors."

"Yes. She worked with them almost exclusively."

"Selling residential and commercial property in the city," Rebecca added.

"Well, she was a realtor," Sean said with a small smile.

"And you were involved with that, how?"

"As a friend, as I already said." He crossed his legs and folded his hands. "She had many investors who wanted to buy homes and businesses in the city. San Francisco is doing phenomenally well these days, with the Silicon Valley people moving here and—"

"I'm aware of the city's allure," she said, interrupting his Chamber of Commerce B.S. "That doesn't answer my question."

"Well," he cleared his throat, "sometimes when there are legal screw-ups a contact in local government can help smooth things over, make them work a lot more smoothly. That's all."

"Someone like you?" she asked.

"Me? No, I'm just a staffer. Audrey never came to me for anything." He folded his hands. "I could point her in the right direction, nothing more."

"I've heard you were involved with her investors," Rebecca said. Even if she hadn't, she might have.

He gave a small laugh. "You heard wrong. Sometimes one of her investors wanted to make a charitable donation to the city and Audrey would ask me who was most in need at the moment."

"A charitable donation? Why?"

He shrugged. "It shows good will towards the city, and that opens doors."

"You spoke to her before midnight last Wednesday night. I can't imagine that was about a donation."

"I did?" He had a sudden deer-in-the-headlights look. "Oh, yes! How could I forget! It was because we had scheduled a nine A.M. meeting the next day to talk about the San Francisco Opera foundation. Do you know we have one of the world's best opera companies? It is truly amazing—"

"You called that late at night about a meeting?" she asked.

"Because it was canceled. And I knew she'd still be awake. I didn't want her to rush over here for an early meeting for no reason. And if she didn't answer, I'd have simply left a message. But I got to speak to her. Who knew that little nothing of a conversation would be the last time." He gave a deep sigh and dropped his gaze to the floor.

"Is your holding company involved with real estate the way hers is?"

"My ... oh, I have money in a trust. That could involve holding companies. I really don't know. I have no head for finances." He gave a forced laugh and was clearly nervous. "I leave all that to my financial counselor."

"I see." She handed him her card as she rose to her feet.

He stood as well, looking relieved that the questioning was over.

"We need to continue this discussion, but we'll do it in Homicide, fourth floor, Hall of Justice," she said. "I'll see you there at nine o'clock tomorrow morning. You don't need to bring your attorney, but you might tell him to be within easy reach." Pressure—especially when it was delivered in a forbidding, scary place such as Homicide's windowless interrogation room —did get some people to buckle and tell all. And Hinkle, she suspected, would be one of them.

He blanched and looked almost faint. "My attorney? I don't understand. Why?"

She just smiled. "See you in the morning, Sean. I'll see myself out." Why, she wondered as she walked away, had she ever gone out with him?

Rebecca hadn't been back at her desk two minutes when Lt. James Philip Eastwood came flying out of his office. "What do you think you're doing?" he bellowed.

"What do you mean?"

"You were questioning an important member of the mayor's staff without telling me?"

"I'm sorry, but it just came up that he was the last person, other than the killer, that I know of who talked to Audrey Poole. Of course I wanted to talk to him."

"And you didn't think to let me know so that when the mayor called up to ask why my detective was wasting her time harassing his staff I'd have at least a prayer of answering him?"

"I was going to brief you now that I'm back."

"Your partner didn't know anything about it either!" Eastwood said, his face truly red now.

She looked around. "Where is Sutter?"

"He said he was going to look for you. I suspect he's hiding."

She waited a moment before she added. "I'm going to formally interview Sean Hinkle tomorrow morning, right here."

Eastwood pursed his lips. "Come into my office. I want to hear everything."

23

After Rebecca calmed Eastwood down and returned to her desk, Sutter reappeared. The two of them reviewed their progress on the two murders. Neither one was pleased with their findings.

Since there was still no answer at the Bay-to-Breakers Realty, Rebecca tracked down the building owner and told him she needed him to let her into the office. He insisted someone was usually there between noon and two. When she pressed, he said he'd meet her at noon.

While Sutter went to Pinocchio's to show a picture of Sean Hinkle to the cocktail waitress who served Audrey Poole and to ask if he was the person Audrey met there, Rebecca drove out to the Noriega Street address. It was a small storefront in a neighborhood shopping area. The building owner was pacing the sidewalk as she approached. "You don't need me to unlock it. Someone's in there, just like I said."

An OPEN sign was in the window and the lights were on. "I see. Thank you for meeting me in any case."

"It's not as if I've got time to come here for no good reason," the man muttered and stormed off.

Rebecca entered. She'd never seen a real estate office as quiet and empty as this.

A young woman sat at a desk with a computer and a phone. A nameplate in front of her read "Heather Louie." Nearby was a small table with a few small bundles of brochures and real estate flyers, and in each corner stood a spindly potted plant, probably fake. Everything seemed to have a sheen of dust over it as if doing anything here would be disturbing history.

Ms. Louie was wearing earphones connected to her smart phone, and was so engrossed in reading, she paid no attention as Rebecca approached.

"Hello," Rebecca said.

The woman looked up, startled. She yanked the earbuds off and shut her e-reader. "My goodness. I'm sorry! I guess I didn't hear the door."

"I guess not." Rebecca showed her badge. "Inspector Mayfield, Homicide."

"Are you looking for a house?" The woman asked with a small smile as if having a homicide detective standing in front of her was an everyday occurrence. She was young, attractive, and looked as if she might be of Chinese descent.

"I'm not here as a client," Rebecca said. "I'm here because of Audrey Poole."

The receptionist's smile never wavered. "Oh, I'm sorry. Ms. Poole isn't in at the moment. Can I take a message and have her call you?"

"I don't think so," Rebecca said, then took a deep breath. She guessed it wasn't really this woman's fault that no one had notified her of what had happened, or that she hadn't heard the news. She also realized how badly she and Sutter had screwed up by ignoring Poole's office for so many days. "You are Heather Louie?" she asked, pointing at the nameplate.

"That's right."

"Your position?"

"Ms. Poole calls me her office manager."

Of course she does. "Have you worked here long?"

"I guess. About three months."

"I see. And who opened up the office for you today?"

"Nobody. Ms. Poole trusts me with her key. It's not as if there's anything here to steal. The computer has a nice looking monitor, but it's just an XP. I didn't think it would even work, but it's connected to the internet, and that's all I ever need. I come in a few hours each week to check on the place, handle mail, deal with emails. That sort of thing."

"I see. Do you keep any files in the office?"

"No. Anything Ms. Poole wants, she picks up. But almost everything is junk mail and gets thrown away."

"Did you have contact with anyone from Bay-to-Breakers today?"

"Only Ms. Poole. I mean, there's no one else here but Ms. Poole. And me, of course."

Rebecca was taken aback. "Wait, are you saying you spoke to Audrey Poole today?"

"No. I rarely talk with her. But I forwarded some emails and typed up her voice messages and emailed them. She does her important work by text or her private number, but she prefers I send emails because most of the calls that come through this office aren't a high priority. They can wait."

"Did you type up messages from Inspector Mayfield, Homicide?"

"Yes, several." Heather's eyes widened as she put two-and-two together. "Oh."

Rebecca's lips tightened. "When did you last actually speak with Ms. Poole?"

"Speak to her? Gee, I'm not sure. Maybe last week."

"So what were the emails you sent today?"

"You mean, you want to see them?"

"That's right," Rebecca said.

Heather opened and shut her mouth a couple of times as if unsure what to say. "Ms. Poole said I should never tell anybody about any of her clients. Not unless she specifically tells me it's all right."

"I see," Rebecca said with a sage nod. "Maybe you can tell me if anyone seemed particularly angry at Ms. Poole. Is there anyone she dealt with that worried you, perhaps? Or maybe even scared you a bit?"

The receptionist's brow formed a worried frown. "Not that I can think of. Why? Is something wrong? Did something happen to Ms. Poole?"

"Try to think if there's anyone troubling to you, please."

Heather bit her bottom lip. "Hmm. Nobody important ever comes into this office. Most people phone. And they just ask to talk to Ms. Poole, you know. Nothing more. I mean, some sound anxious, like they're in a hurry. But not angry."

"Tell me," Rebecca said, "are you by any chance Chinese?"

"Yes." Ms. Louie smiled. "Ms. Poole does a lot of work with China. Every so often she asks me to translate something for her. Or to talk on the phone to someone in Shanghai. She mostly deals with Shanghai—lots of money there. She said she'll take me with her the next time she goes."

Hearing that, Rebecca decided it was time to come clean. "I'm sorry to tell you, I'm here because I have some bad news."

Heather paled. "Yes?"

"Ms. Poole was attacked Wednesday night on the street near her home. I'm afraid she didn't survive."

"Didn't survive?" Heather whispered, then stood up. "She's dead?"

Rebecca nodded. "Now, I need you to think very clearly. Is there anyone at all who might have wanted to harm Ms. Poole?"

"I don't know. She seemed as if everyone liked her. Oh, my!" She sat down again and stared up at Rebecca, her eyes filled with tears. "That's terrible. I liked her. It would have been so neat to travel with her."

"I'm sorry," Rebecca said. It seemed she was saying that a lot lately. "I'll be sending some computer experts from CSI to go through your computer. They'll contact you shortly to make sure you're here when they arrive."

"Okay," Heather murmured.

"Here's my card. Call me if you think of anything that might help."

With that, she placed her business card on the desk and walked out of the office. She was about to turn towards her SUV when she noticed someone familiar sitting in a pickup parked across the street. She stared. The person scrunched down and turned his head away.

She walked up to the pickup's passenger door, and when it wouldn't open, knocked on the window. "Open up, Vito."

"Inspector! What a surprise!" He sat up and unlocked the door. "I was trying to find some good music on the radio and didn't see you."

"Sure you were," she said and got into the car beside him. "Why does Richie have you watching Audrey Poole's office?"

"Uh..."

"Out with it."

"He wanted me to see if anyone takes over for Ms. Poole."

She nodded. "And?"

"No one."

"Why does he care who takes over?"

"It might be something about his mother. I'm not sure," Vito said. And from his tone, he didn't want to know. Thinking about Richie's mother, Rebecca didn't blame him.

"Who have you seen entering or leaving the office?"

"Besides the secretary, only one person. You. And I been here three days now. But the place is mostly closed. The girl, I mean, young lady, shows up a couple hours a day, weekdays only from what I've seen. Then she leaves, and so do I."

"Okay, thanks. I told her Audrey Poole is dead. No one contacted her, apparently, and I guess she doesn't bother with local news. CSI will show up for her computer, and after that, I expect she won't be back."

"Thanks for letting me know, Inspector," Vito said.

Rebecca opened the door to get out of the truck when he added, "Wait, Inspector. Can we talk?"

She glanced at him. He looked worried and more hang-dog than ever. "Sure." She pulled the door shut.

His brows crossed, and he put both hands on the steering wheel as if he had to steel himself to talk to her.

She waited.

"I don't mean to take up your time when you're working," he said, "but I'm worried about the boss."

She knew he meant Richie. "You mean because of this case? Have you guys learned something I need to know about Audrey Poole or her business?

"No. You don't get it. Me and Shay can keep him safe. That's not what I'm worried about."

"Okay..." She waited.

He glanced at her, then the top of the truck, then the steering wheel, and finally back at her. "You see, well, he's not been himself lately. He's miserable. Not eating much. Cranky as all get-out. And also, Shay isn't himself. Plus, he's paying a lot of attention to you and your work schedule, and I know you and him have worked together in the past."

The more Rebecca heard Vito say, the more astonished she was becoming. He couldn't be implying what it sounded like. "Vito, what are you talking about?"

He seemed to grit his teeth. "I was wondering if you and Shay—"

"Stop!" She all but shuddered. "Me and Shay? Are you joking?" She couldn't tell Vito, but she found Shay too weird for words. "No way!"

"But you're both real good with guns and kind of think alike."

"We do?" That actually worried her. From all she'd seen, Shay was a borderline sociopath. She didn't know what to say.

"Thank God, I was wrong, Inspector. I didn't think you two would get together, but I couldn't help but remember that Dante said, 'The more souls resonate together, the greater the intensity of their love,' so I thought—"

"I don't think he meant being snipers together," she snapped. She was getting to dislike Vito's Dante quotes almost as much as Richie did. "You don't think Richie imagines there's anything between me and Shay, do you?"

Vito's face scrunched up. "Nah. I don't think so. He keeps getting mad at Shay, but he picks on me, too, and he sure as hell doesn't think we're—" with that, he blushed to the top of his receding hairline. Rebecca didn't think men who were tough and pushy, in other words "muscle," the way Vito could be when necessary, could still blush. Obviously, she was wrong.

"Anyway," Vito continued, "all I can say is, I don't know what's going on with those two guys. I love 'em like brothers, but I wish they'd both marry and settle down. Then they'd be easier to understand."

Vito had, again, rendered her speechless.

He continued. "I guess you and the boss ain't seeing eye-to-eye these days, huh? Splitsville?"

"Who knows?" Rebecca said. "You know how these things go."

"I'm sure sorry to hear that, Inspector."

She opened the door and got out of the truck. "Thanks, Vito. You take care of those two—sounds like they both need you right now."

As she headed back to her SUV, she replayed Vito's strange conversation in her mind.

She walked around his truck and seeing the street clear, started to jaywalk.

Suddenly, she felt a ham-like arm wrap around her waist. She was about to fight it when she saw the ugly brown of the coat sleeve covering that arm. Vito? He easily lifted her off her feet, spun around and tossed her towards the sidewalk. His big bulk stood between her and the street for just an instant when he lunged forward, knocking them both to the ground between two parked cars as a black sedan sped by the spot where she would have been standing had he not grabbed her.

Vito had left the truck door open as he rushed to pull her out of harm's way, and the sedan drove so close it hit the truck's door and knocked it off its hinges and into the air. The sedan didn't stop, but kept going.

Rebecca watched, stunned and breathless from the close call. "Where did it come from? I didn't see it."

"It's been circling the street ever since you showed up here, and then it parked," Vito said. "As you started to cross, I saw it pull out of the parking space. I figured what was up."

"Thank you, Vito," she murmured.

"You got to be careful, Inspector. The boss thinks something weird is going on here. And now, I'd say he's right."

Richie, Vito and Shay sat in Richie's favorite booth at the Leaning Tower Taverna. Vito had called Richie after witnessing

Rebecca's close call out on Noriega Street, and Richie wanted to meet to talk about it.

"You need to stick with her, boss, day and night," Vito suggested. "You done it before."

Richie hated to bend the truth to his best friends, but the open looks on their faces, from Vito's dark eyes to Shay's luminous blue ones, made him realize he couldn't yet tell them what was really going on.

"I can't," he murmured.

"What do you mean?" Shay asked.

"Well ... I'm not sure how much I'll be seeing her." Richie blurted the words fast. It was the only way he could get them out.

"Shit," Vito muttered, casting a bleak eye towards Shay.

"Christ, Richie!" Shay's brows crossed. "You're crazy about her. What's wrong with you?"

Richie leaned back. He didn't want to talk about it, but he also knew the guys wouldn't give up. He couldn't tell them she was walking out on him. It didn't fit his love'em-and-leave'em image, and at the moment, image was all he had left.

Finally, he fell back on his mother's words, much as he hated himself for doing it. "It's complicated."

Shay said nothing, but Vito exclaimed, "Yeah, the Inspector said pretty much the same thing."

"You talked to Rebecca about me?" Richie bellowed.

"Not much, boss," Vito said. "I thought something was wrong, but I wasn't sure, that's all. I mean, it looked like you guys was getting along great, and then *poof.*"

Richie decided he owed it to them to try to explain. "I care about her. Still do; a lot. But nothing's going to come of it. You know it, I know it, and Rebecca knows it. I need to find someone to marry and settle down. I'm staring forty in the face. It's time. I used to hate hearing my mother tell me that because I thought she was wrong. Now, I hate it because I know she's right. Even about the grandkids she wants to spoil rotten."

"So marry Rebecca." Vito's arms spread so wide he could have been announcing a solution for world peace.

"Yeah, like that's going to happen." Richie scoffed. "Apparently, the one and only time she forgot herself and kissed me in front of some other cops, she was ribbed so much about it she went around work telling anyone who'd listen that she was temporarily carried away with relief that I was alive. And that the public display of emotion meant nothing at all."

"She told you that?" Shay asked.

"No. My cousin Angie told me she heard it from her husband. Paavo wasn't there at the time, but when he went back to Homicide the next day, all the inspectors were talking about it. That was Rebecca's explanation for what's going on between us."

"She was just trying to get them off her back," Vito said. "You know how guys are."

"For all I know, it might be best if she dates other guys." He tried not to spit out the words. "Get some perspective, or whatever."

"Really? You wouldn't care?" Vito asked.

Like hell, I wouldn't! "I'd get over it."

"How does she feel?" Shay asked.

"I suspect the same way." Richie took a long swallow of his glass of Anchor Steam, then faced his friends. "Besides that, she's ambitious. She probably sees herself as becoming chief of police someday. And frankly, as a smart woman and a good cop, she has a decent chance of it. I don't exactly have the best résumé for the role of a police chief's spouse."

Vito's mouth wrinkled. "The picture you're painting isn't the woman I seen around you."

"Come on, Vito. You know we're like oil and water," Richie

said. "We don't mix, okay? Besides, she's practical to a fault, and probably has already figured out that she'll need to marry someone in the law—preferably someone in the district attorney's office. Or, maybe a judge."

"If you really believed that of her," Shay said, "you'd never bother to see her again."

Richie wished Shay wasn't so good at calling his bluff. "Maybe," he admitted.

"You gotta roll the dice, boss," Vito said. "Sometimes you get snake eyes, but you could also roll a seven or eleven. But let the game play out."

Richie looked at Vito a long moment. That was actually damn good advice. Maybe there was something to reading all that Dante as a kid. "I'll think about it," he said finally. "But none of this means we shouldn't all keep an eye on her. Just that we won't tell her we're doing it."

24

Later that night, since Big Caesars was closed on Mondays, Richie was home when his phone buzzed. Usually he had lots to do, people to see, and fun to be had. Tonight he didn't want to do anything at all. The TV was on, but he couldn't find a single game that interested him, and he had every sports package available. He sat facing it, alone and miserable.

"Something's going on, boss," Vito said into the phone when Richie roused himself enough to answer. Vito sounded breathless and tense. "I was keeping an eye on the Inspector's house like we said I should. Since it's nearly midnight, I was thinking everything was okay, when she comes out of the house and gets in her car. I got the police band on my shortwave, and there's nothing going on about a homicide. I'm saying, when a body's found, it's big, and there's a lot of chatter."

It took a moment for Richie to put all the pieces Vito was saying together, but once he did, he didn't like it. "Where are you?" he asked. "What's she doing?"

"She's heading west on Geary. Towards the Richmond district. She had her firearm. I don't think she's going out for pizza."

"I'll call Shay. We'll follow."

"It could be nothing, boss," Vito said. "I don't want to take you from your home on a hunch, but I thought I'd call, just in case."

"Your hunches are better than most. I'm coming."

Richie hung up. He had a bad feeling about Vito's call. From the time he learned that both Sean Hinkle—in other words, City Hall—as well as a Chinese triad might be involved in Audrey's real estate dealings, he'd been worried about Rebecca. San Francisco politics was always a rough game, and some people, particularly those on the fringes, weren't the up-and-up types they liked to convince voters they were. None of them would stand for one lone detective ruining all they had going.

He tried to call Rebecca. She didn't answer. She often didn't take any personal calls when she was headed for a crime scene. She'd been taught the importance of leaving the phone line open.

He got into his Porsche and headed north. From the car, he called Shay who lived in the Presidio Heights area. "Rebecca just went out on a call that Vito finds suspicious. They're heading west on Geary, in your direction. I'm going that way, but if you're home, you're a lot closer."

"I'm home. I'll call Vito and head out right now."

Vito phoned back to say Rebecca had turned off Geary to go north on 25th Avenue. Richie knew a shortcut through Golden Gate Park to that area and took it.

He tried to reach Rebecca again, with no more luck than his last call.

He gave her a chance to call him back, but when she didn't, he contacted Vito once more. "What's happening now?"

"She pulled into the Baker's Beach parking lot. I left my truck out on the street and I'm hiding back among in the trees and shrubs watching her, but it's so damned foggy out here, I can't see much of anything. No other cops though. I don't know why she's here."

"It's not good," Richie said. "I wonder if she's trying to meet someone connected with this case, someone like Sean Hinkle."

"Who?"

"Nothing. Just tell me what you see."

"Hold on." Vito was whispering now. "She's walking around. Let me get closer. I'll call you back."

Richie felt he was hitting every red light as he went. He called Shay to let him know what was happening.

A short while later, Vito phoned. "Sorry, boss. False alarm. Another cop showed up. He told her she's the first one here, that the crime scene is at the north end of the beach. He said the uniforms are parked up the road, that they took a path down the hillside, which you know is plenty steep. The Inspector's taking the beach to get there."

"Make sure the cops are where they're supposed to be," Richie said. "I'm almost there and this still doesn't feel right."

Richie immediately hung up and called Shay, explaining everything to him.

"I'm just turning onto Lincoln," Shay said. "I'll forget the parking area and head up the hill. There are a few paths down to the beach. Hold on, I'm almost there."

Richie waited, and in a minute Shay came back. "No squad cars anywhere around here."

"Damn! Are you sure?"

"I'm sure. Vito just showed up. He's been driving around, too, but he couldn't find any cops either. I'm heading down to the beach."

"Okay," Richie said. "I'll be right behind you."

Vito was waiting by the side of the road when Richie arrived, his truck behind Shay's Maserati. "I screwed up, boss. I'm sorry. I should've followed her on the beach," Vito said.

"Take this." He handed Richie his Glock as Richie got out of the car.

Richie looked over the weapon. The magazine was full. "We'll make it right, Vito. Don't worry."

"Shay went down what they call a 'sand ladder.' It's right over there," Vito said. "I never been down it, so I don't know how tough it might be."

"It's better than nothing, I'm sure," Richie said.

He sent a text to Shay, and then took the steep, slippery path to the beach.

Shay met him at the bottom. "I checked this area. The fog is brutal, but I'm pretty sure she's not here. Let's head north."

Richie was fuming as they went. He was the one who had pulled Vito off Rebecca's trail. He should have known better. And now, in this thick fog, he wondered if they'd ever find her. One thing he knew for certain, they weren't looking for a crime scene. Out here was just Rebecca ... and whoever it was that wanted her here alone.

He had to find her; he couldn't lose her, too.

He and Shay were almost at the rocks when he heard a hail of gunshots. That was no handgun, he thought. It sounded like a semi-automatic rifle. His heart in his throat, he and Shay ran towards the sound.

Towards the rocks.

As quickly as it began, all became silent. Richie wouldn't let himself think what that might mean—that Rebecca wasn't able to fight back. He would find her. She would be safe.

There was silence for a while, and then a single shot. Almost immediately, it was followed by another barrage, and then what sounded like hand-gun fire coming from the cliffs.

"I suspect it's Rebecca near the cliffs," Shay said. "I'll go after the one with the assault rifle."

Richie nodded. He was slinking towards the cliff he heard

more shots from the direction Shay had gone, followed by a fusillade of bullets. When he realized they were falling near him, he dropped to the sand, hands over his head as bullets flew.

He scrambled towards the cliffs as gunfire continued.

"Rebecca?" he called softly.

"Richie?" she whispered.

He followed the sound of her voice. "I can't see a damned thing out here."

"Stay down," she said.

"I see the cliffs," Richie said.

"I don't ... Ah! I can make out your form. Move a little to your right, and straight."

More gunfire was heard, and Richie ran towards her. She grabbed his jacket and pulled him into the concave section where she'd been hiding, and then even closer.

The gunfire stopped.

He put his hands on her waist. "You okay?" he asked.

She continued to hold his jacket and nodded.

"You should have answered your damned phone," he said, his heart in his throat.

She nodded again. Up close, he could see her eyes dart with fright, her face all but drained of color. "I don't know where the shooter is, or what's going on out here." Her words were a whisper.

"Shay's gone after him."

"Shay, thank God!" She glanced quickly at her firearm. "I'm almost out of bullets, and I don't think I hit him at all."

Richie thought about holding her closer, but then he froze, scarcely breathing. "I heard something," he whispered.

He let her go, and both pressed themselves against the cliff's wall, peering in the direction of the water. Rebecca stood ready to fire her gun. Richie knelt, peering around her, also staring hard at the beach and trying to see what was out there. He held

Vito's Glock. He wasn't a good shot, but he could pull a damned trigger if he needed to.

"Don't shoot!" Shay said as he ran towards them. "I'm pretty sure the shooter was hit, but I don't know where he is or how badly he's hurt. I suggest we get out of here while we can."

"Wait," Rebecca murmured as she began to pick up her shell casings. She was moving slowly as if still in shock from the way she'd been targeted. Richie helped her and stuffed all the casings into his own pocket. If someone reported the shoot-out, they could have been traced back to her and her gun.

He took hold of her arm, and with Shay leading the way, the three climbed back up the sand ladder to their cars.

"Give Vito your car keys," Richie said to Rebecca. "He'll drive your SUV. If someone tries to follow it, he knows how to lose any tail. Then, he'll hide it."

"Hide it?" she asked. He could tell she was still rattled by the shoot-out.

"So whoever was trying to kill you will think you got away—far away," Richie explained. "It'll buy us some time."

She hung back. "But ..."

"We don't know how many are looking for you. That shooter might be calling for back-up. Now, move!" He knew he sounded harsh, but he had to get through to her. She was the one in danger now.

Zombie-like, she got into the Porsche's passenger seat, and Richie drove off.

Instead of driving to his house, Richie pulled into the alleyway behind Big Caesar's. They entered through the back door. Rebecca said little as he drove, but he essentially got her to explain about her call from the dispatcher and being sent out along the beach.

"Why are we here?" Rebecca asked when she saw where they were.

"It's safer than my house," Richie said. "If whoever did this is able to make you think they were dispatch telling you to go out on a call, and had someone dressed up like a cop to fool you even more, they're plenty clever. And it's not just one person. More like, I hate to say it, but like a gang that could have ties to city government. And if so, they know where you live and where I live. They'll be looking for you at your place, and depending on how much they know about us, possibly at mine."

They went into his office. Richie handed her a shot of brandy. She downed it in one gulp. Richie didn't drink anything, instead he watched her. "Sit down, Rebecca," he said, gesturing towards the sofa. "You're white as a sheet."

She did as told. "I couldn't believe what was happening. I've never been a target like that."

"You're sniffing around City Hall, Chinese triads, and powerful foreign investors," Richie said, "all of whom can have ties to unsavory characters. People who don't give a damn about body counts. Someone doesn't want you to get any closer. What's going on here is potentially huge, and we don't know how deep it goes."

"That could mean you're in danger, too."

"Yes, it could," Richie murmured, then got up and put his jacket back on. "Get some rest. You'll think better in the morning. This place is like a fortress. I'll make sure everything's okay, and I'll leave you alone. Shay's outside keeping an eye on the place. You'll be safe."

"You're leaving?" She hated that her voice still sounded small and frightened.

"Would you like company?" he asked.

She was tempted to say she did, but he looked antsy, as if he had things to do but didn't want to tell her. "I'll be fine," she murmured.

"Good. I've got a couple of things to take care of, then I'll be back."

Who could argue with "things" to do at two in the morning? "Before you go," she said, "thank you for helping me. But how did you even know I was out there?"

"You can thank Vito," he said with a gentle smile. "He wanted to keep an eye on you tonight after the incident on Noriega Street. He followed when you went out and also called me. Vito's intuition has saved me more than once. I contacted Shay, and the rest, you pretty much know."

She shut her eyes, thinking she likely would be on her way to the morgue now if Vito hadn't been suspicious. When Richie, Shay, and Vito had shown up, she was down to only a few bullets left, and from the fusillades that were fired at her, whoever was trying to kill her had come well armed. "It was so scary," she muttered.

"Yes, it was." Richie then showed Rebecca the cellar and places to hide if she needed to. Last, he showed her a side door that led to the alley. If it came to that, he directed her to run.

He was about to step out of the club to his car when she put her hand on his shoulder.

Surprised, he turned back to her. She put her arms around his shoulders and held him tight. His arms circled her and they remained that way a long time.

Then, he left.

~

Richie drove to Mulford Alley and rang the doorbell to Rebecca's landlord's flat several times.

About five minutes passed before he heard Bradley Frick's voice on the other side of the door. "Who's there?"

"Richie Amalfi, Rebecca's friend."

Bradley opened the door, his eyebrows raised, and a frightened, questioning expression on his face. "What is it?"

"Rebecca needs your help."

"My help?" He was dressed in p.j.s and a bathrobe, his bleached blond hair askew, making the spikes look more like bent nails. "What's going on? First Kiki, now Rebecca? This neighborhood has become a war zone!"

Richie pushed his way into the flat and shut the door behind him. He didn't want to be caught outside if whoever had tried to kill Rebecca showed up at her apartment sooner than he expected. Bradley's eyes went round, gawking at Richie as if he were crazy. They stood at the bottom of a long flight of stairs that led up to Bradley's top-floor flat.

"Don't worry," Richie said. "Rebecca's going undercover for a while. All she asks is that you take care of Spike for her. And if anyone comes here looking for her, even if they say they're the police, don't believe it and don't tell them you've got her dog. Only say you haven't seen her and you have no idea where she is. Got it?"

"Even the police?" Bradley looked ready to pass out.

"Tell yourself they could be fake, okay?"

"But badges—"

"You haven't seen her and have no idea where she is. Repeat that."

Bradley swallowed hard and murmured the words, his voice as thin and shaky as a ninety-year-old's.

"Also, if they see Spike, just say he's your dog."

"Why?" Bradley's voice was just a squeak.

"They need to think she's run off. If they see her dog, they'll assume you know where she is, and that won't be good for you."

"Oh, my."

"Got it?"

He gave a quick, slight nod. "I got it."

Richie made sure no one was watching and then ran out of Mulford Alley to the street two blocks away where he'd parked.

A half hour later he was home. He had been tempted to go back to Big Caesar's to stay with Rebecca, but knew it would be better if he didn't. Besides, anyone looking for her would more likely show up at his place than at the nightclub.

He changed into sweats and sat in the living room with muted baseball highlight films on the TV, and the Glock at his side. He didn't plan to sleep that night.

25

R ebecca lay on the couch in Richie's office. She had tried to sleep, but her mind raced with visions of the beach.

She sat up, instantly wide awake, at the sound of footsteps in the hallway. She picked up her SIG Sauer as the doorknob turned. It was Richie.

She relaxed and put the weapon down. "What time is it?" she asked.

"Six."

She rubbed her eyes. "Ugh! I'm surprised you're already awake."

"I haven't been to sleep yet."

Her face fell at the implication of danger behind his words. "I've got to go home. I can't leave Spike alone with no food or fresh water."

"No problem. I visited your landlord last night. He's taking care of Spike."

Rebecca could only gape at that. Bradley liked Spike and would take good care of him but she could only imagine how he reacted to a visit from Richie. She had somehow managed to keep the two apart up to this point. Bradley was the type who easily felt intimidated and Richie could be imposing under the best of circumstances. And particularly when he was making a "request," he came across as someone you might not want to say no to. "Thank you," she said. "I appreciate you thinking about him."

"I'd have taken him myself, except I'm not sure where this will lead. Spike is safe with Bradley."

"You're right," she murmured.

"Now, let's get out of here."

"Get out? Where are we going?"

"Some place no one will think of."

She needed a minute to put her boots back on and freshen up. She looked longingly at the shower, but knew that was a luxury she definitely didn't have time for. That didn't stop her from wondering why he'd installed a shower in the office bathroom, but that was a question for another day.

He had parked in the alley behind the building. The sun was just beginning to light the sky as they crept out the back door and jumped in the Porsche. As they drove, she called Homicide. No one was there this early, as she expected, so she left a message for both Eastwood and Sutter that she woke up with a bad case of stomach flu and wouldn't be in that day, but that she hoped to see them tomorrow.

Richie drove to Chinatown and pulled into a brick-lined alley that dead-ended.

"Are you kidding?" she asked as they got out.

"Nope."

He led her to a door that opened as they approached. She recognized the Chinese man who opened it. "You remember Benny Wong," Richie said.

"Of course." She wondered why they were there.

"Inspector," Benny said with a slight bow, "don't worry. We'll take good care of you. Richie explained everything to me."

"Thank you, but there must be some mistake." She faced Richie. "I can't stay here. I'm not about to hide. I've got to find out what's going on."

"You will. We all will, but not when you've got a target on your back."

"We'll head downstairs," Benny said, leading them to a stairway. "The room is big enough for two, by the way. And I won't bother you. It's under the restaurant, so when you need food, you just go on up. We'll make a plate to take back downstairs. That way, you won't be hungry."

"Under the restaurant?" Rebecca looked at Richie as they went down two flights of stairs.

"Where else?" Richie murmured.

"You know those tunnels and underground passageways you were always told existed in Chinatown?" Benny said, having heard Rebecca's words.

"Yes," she said.

"They really do exist," Benny said as they reached the bottom of the stairs and were in a small hallway. "You go through that door"—he pointed to one with a deadbolt—"and you'll be in one of the tunnels. If you are scared about something, just go through it and then run. Eventually, you'll find a way out. I can't say where—it all depends on the turns you make as you run."

"Thanks," she said. "But I don't intend to run from anyone."

Benny's dark eyes glanced in Richie's direction.

"Don't blame me," Richie said to him, both hands raised. "I had nothing to do with this."

"Not this time, at least," Rebecca added.

The two were shown to a small room with a double bed, chair, dresser, small refrigerator, hot plate, tea kettle, and a bathroom with an old, rusting tub and no shower. It made her wish for Richie's place all the more. The walls were a kind of dark cream color, which Rebecca suspected had been nearly white some twenty or thirty years ago when they were last painted. The furniture wouldn't have been accepted by Goodwill.

"I'll leave you two." Benny walked out of the room and shut the door behind him.

"Home sweet home." Richie muttered as even he looked dismayed by the space. "At least you'll be safe here." He walked to the bed and pushed down on the mattress. The springs squealed so loudly it was like something straight out of an old Laurel and Hardy comedy. "I'm going to check out that tunnel."

She went out into the dingy hallway with him.

Richie went to the door, unlocked and opened it. Both he and Rebecca looked in at what was a narrow passage framed with wood. It had no lighting, and apparently no electricity. "I don't think I'll be using that," Richie said firmly.

"I wonder if it has rats." Rebecca took a couple of steps inside, but then stopped.

"There are rats all over the city," Richie replied, "especially as you get near the wharves. Did you know there was once bubonic plague in the city? It was a hundred years ago, but seemed to be centered in Chinatown."

"Do you have to tell me that now?" Her voice a little too high, she scurried back to the hallway. Rats were bad enough, but plague?

He chuckled. "Sorry. It was eradicated and never came back ... I don't think."

"You can stop anytime. There's no way in hell I'm going into that tunnel, so I don't care of Godzilla's in there."

"Want me to check it out for you?" he asked.

She was tempted to say yes, but that would have been mean. "Oh, right, like you'd do that," she said. "You go in there and start crying for help, you're on your own, buddy."

He smirked, but as she looked at his humor-filled expression, she realized that, like her, he was glad for the chance to banter, to ease a little of the tension of the past few hours, as well as the tension between them.

They hurried back to the room Benny had given them.

Rebecca sat on one side of the bed. Not only did the mattress squeal and sag, but a big puff of dust rose from it.

"Take one side of this bedspread," Richie said as he took the other. Together, they brought it out to the hallway and shook it, then hurried back inside and shut the door so the dust wouldn't blow back in. They folded it up and put it atop the bureau.

Having the bedspread off gave Rebecca a chance to check out the blanket, pillowcases and sheets to make sure there were no creepy-crawly bugs or other critters living in there. There weren't. Not under the bed, either. She suspected any mice nearby probably didn't bother with that room since there was no food in it.

"I think this is a keep-your-socks-on kind of place," Rebecca said woefully.

Richie looked down at the bed, and then over at the small, spindly chair. He sat on the bed. "Kind of depressing, isn't it?"

"This entire situation is." She sat on the opposite side.

"Why don't you lie down and get back to sleep. You're going to need to be sharp to deal with all this. I'll be right here. You don't have to worry."

"You need some sleep as well," she said.

"I'm fine."

"But we should be doing something, not hiding out in Chinatown."

"At this time in the morning?"

She realized she'd barely slept in his office as she'd been worried about everything that had happened on the fog drenched beach. Now, in the quiet of this strange but safe little room, a bone-aching weariness came over her and she stretched out on the bed. The mattress seemed to sag nearly to the floor.

She was about to tell him she didn't think she could fall asleep, given the danger, but she must have dozed off before she could say a word.

A nightmare, a dream of her trying to run on the beach but being slowed down because of soft sand sucking at her shoes, of being hunted, and then, of a man with an assault rifle standing in front of her, raising his gun to shoot, startled her awake.

She looked around the dark room. It took a moment to remember where she was, and then to shift from the near-reality of the dream to being here, underground in Chinatown. Her breath came in small, quivering waves.

Beside her, on his side, his back to her and snoring lightly, was Richie. The way the mattress sagged in the middle under both their weights, she was close to him. She could have tried to ease away, but she didn't. Instead she turned on her side, facing him, and rested her arm against his back, glad she wasn't alone when the nightmare hit. Glad he and his friends had looked for her. As much as she liked to think she could have gotten away from the gunman, she honestly didn't know. But she did know the chance of getting away unscathed was slim to none.

She noticed, then, that his deep, sleep-filled breathing had stopped. It was almost as if he were holding his breath. A part of her—most of her—was tempted to whisper his name. She was certain that one simple word, any word, would have gotten him to turn and face her. She knew where that would lead—exactly where she wanted it to.

If she were the type of woman who could separate loving a man with her body from the feelings she had for him in her mind, she would have done so. But she couldn't.

She shut her eyes, not daring to move, and prayed for the oblivion of sleep.

26

When Rebecca awoke, she was alone on the bed. Richie had left a note saying he'd meet her in the restaurant at noon, and that he would call Shay and Vito to join them.

She stepped into the Jade Dragon's dining room.

Richie sat at a table in the back, next to the kitchen—an easy exit if necessary. She was glad he decided to meet here, where there were windows and daylight, rather than in the private downstairs room where they usually dined.

She joined him.

She no sooner sat than Shay walked in, his blue-eyed gaze going from her to Richie and back. She was surprised that his stare wasn't as icy as usual. She must be wrong, she told herself. In the months she had known him he never showed the slightest modicum of human compassion. He might be handsome and intelligent, with an ability with software that should be the envy of the NSA, not to mention his skill as a sniper, but he always made her nervous. Still did, come to think of it.

"Shay, I didn't get a chance to thank you for getting me out of there last night," Rebecca said as he sat at the table with them.

"No problem," he said. "But I'll be better as soon as we get to whoever was behind all that."

Vito was right behind him. He greeted everyone and sat, still wearing his heavy tan jacket.

"Vito," Rebecca said smiling at him, "I hear if it weren't for you, I'd probably be 'swimming with the fishes.'"

"Aw," he muttered, his round, fleshy face scrunching into a big but self-deprecating smile. "Just doin' my job."

Rebecca reached over and gave his hand a squeeze.

"Now that we're all here," Richie said. "We've got to figure out who's behind this and stop them. I've never come across anything quite like this." He gave the other two a quick run-down of all Rebecca had experienced on the beach.

"The most troubling was that someone could so realistically fake being a police dispatcher," Rebecca said. "From the way the call looked on my phone, to the type of voice used, everything."

"Let me see your phone," Shay said. She logged in and handed it over.

"It's got to be someone close to government," she continued. "A former cop, or someone who knows a lot of cops and can talk to them using the right jargon, even the rapid-fire but cold, staccato way dispatch sounds when giving instructions."

"That means you've scared someone," Richie said.

"It's a clone," Shay said, giving Rebecca back her phone. "Just like spam can mimic the looks of a real bank or PayPal or whatever, this person mimicked the look of the dispatch calls. But under the shell that showed up on your phone, it went to a website—one of those internet voice phone sites. Most likely it's been bounced around the globe and back several times to hide the place of origin."

"So whoever is behind this knows government, and has serious tech skills," Richie said.

Shay nodded.

"Let's go over what we know," Rebecca said. "Audrey Poole was head of an offshore holding company that buys real estate for foreign investors. She was working with many such investors and was getting help from city officials to do it. Probably all of them were sharing in the profits. One of her big projects was being held up by Kiki Nuñez. Kiki was attacked, her assistant killed."

Rebecca continued. "We know Audrey got a phone call from the mayor's chief of staff, Sean Hinkle, at eleven o'clock Wednesday night. She was seen at the Pinocchio Bar after that with a man, but the man wasn't Hinkle. Sutter brought a picture of Hinkle to the cocktail waitress who remembered seeing Audrey at the bar. The waitress didn't recognize Hinkle as the man with her. She thought he was older, for one thing. The bartender, too, didn't remember seeing Hinkle in the place."

The three men nodded at that bit of new information.

"Two hours later," Rebecca continued, "Audrey was stabbed to death on the street a half-block from her condo—probably by someone she knew since there was no evidence of her putting up any defense, and the stab wounds were from the front, not behind. So who killed her? Was it Hinkle who probably knew she was at the bar and would walk home? Was it the man she was with, or someone else? And *why* was she killed?"

All of them shook their heads.

"I also have two new pieces of information," Shay said. "First, Audrey Poole's accountant drove off a cliff onto the rocky beach below in Sonoma County on Friday night. The authorities up there decided it was a single car accident although everyone swore she was a very careful driver. The few friends she had said she seemed to become very nervous after hearing Audrey Poole had been murdered and was going to a little house up the coast until things quieted down in the city. But she never made it."

"Christ," Richie said. "Somebody's even more desperate than we thought."

Rebecca shuddered, thinking how close she had come to being another victim of whatever was going on in this case.

"And also," Shay said, "I looked into Sean Hinkle. He was in financial trouble. It looks like when the market heated up in the city, he tried setting up an offshore holding company like Audrey's, but he completely messed everything up and ended up owing a lot of big players money. It seems he was trying to put pressure on Audrey to help him get out from under. But she must have refused because it never happened."

"So Hinkle might have killed her out of fury or spite," Rebecca said, "but why go after Inga and Audrey? Not to mention me?"

"Do women talk to their masseuses in the same way as they do with their hairdressers?" Richie asked. "Maybe Audrey said something to Inga that scared Hinkle and he decided both needed silencing."

"It's possible," Rebecca said. "But I used to know Sean fairly well and I just don't see him as a crazed killer. A crook, yes, but a killer, no."

"People change," Richie said, "and who knows what kind of pressure he was under."

"The fact that Audrey was a customer at Kiki's spa must be connected to the attacks on Kiki and Inga," Rebecca said. "But I'm not seeing a clear motive yet."

"Does Kiki know Sean Hinkle?" Shay asked.

"She does like to talk about important people who go to her spa, and she does have a male clientele for the massages, but I don't remember her ever mentioning him," Rebecca said. "Although, she did once tell me the mayor's wife went to her a couple of times for the works."

Shay and Richie caught each other's eyes and quickly looked way.

"What?" Rebecca asked.

When neither man answered, Vito said, "They're thinking about the mayor's wife, and then thinking, 'Didn't help.'"

Richie grinned at that but continued to say nothing.

"Well, anyway," Rebecca said, after giving them a withering stare, "I believe if we can find out why Kiki was a victim, we might be able to figure out who's behind it. I need to try to talk to her again."

"You cannot go waltzing into that hospital," Richie said. "It's the first place whoever is trying to kill you will be watching. In fact, it's time to say the hell with this. Let Sutter figure it out. We can find a place to hide out a while. Or you, alone, if you'd prefer. I know someone with an empty house on an island near Seattle, and—"

"No. I'm a cop, Richie. If you think I'm going to spend any more time hiding—"

"I think," Vito interrupted, his eyes darting between Rebecca and Richie, "I think I might have a solution so you both are happy. For a little while, at least."

Complements of Vito's cousin, Rebecca dressed in a nurse's dark blue smock, matching blue slacks and white shoes. Richie bought her a wig of dark brown hair and also had the presence of mind to include a dark brown eyebrow pencil and mascara. Last of all, he gave her a hospital badge to wear on a cord around her neck. It read "Nurse Amy Caldwell."

"Is that Vito's cousin's name?" she asked.

"Hell, no. If you get caught, she doesn't want anyone to look her way. I didn't ask where she got it, but if she's like Vito, it belongs to someone she hates and wouldn't mind seeing get into trouble."

"Vendetta," Rebecca said.

"See, you do know some Italian!"

When she finished dressing and then putting on the wig and eye make-up, she stepped back. She found it startling to see herself looking so very different, except for the big blue eyes and pointy chin. She never wore bangs, but the wig had bangs that hung down to her now darkened eyebrows. The rest of it was in a straight bob that reached her jaw line.

She took a deep breath. She could do this.

Richie drove her to the hospital and then waited in the car. Someone might recognize him, he said, but not her.

Just inside the hospital entrance, Rebecca found a stack of newspapers. She picked them up, trying to look important, as if she'd been assigned to judiciously dole out the papers to patients. She prayed there would be no medical emergency while she was in a hospital ward. The last thing she wanted was to endanger anyone.

She went straight to Kiki's room.

Kiki was alone, her eyes shut.

"Kiki, how are you doing?" Rebecca said softly.

Kiki opened her eyes, but looked confused for just a moment. Then she smiled. "Becca! Look at you! Oh, my. I thought I was hearing things."

Rebecca couldn't help but smile. "I'm undercover." Richie had told her he'd used that excuse with Bradley Frick. It was as good as any she could think of. "How do you feel? What do your doctors say?"

"I'm getting better. The surgery saved the day. But healing takes so much time. I'm bored to death. Any luck finding out who did this? And who killed Inga?"

"Not yet," Rebecca admitted. "But I'm hoping you can help.

Do you know a man named Sean Hinkle? Or if Inga ever dated a man by that name?"

"Hinkle? No. I never heard of him."

"He works in City Hall, in the mayor's office."

"Inga doesn't like the mayor," Kiki said. "If she was dating one of his people, she'd have told me."

Rebecca agreed with that reasoning. "I've got more questions about Audrey Poole. Do you remember when you last saw her? Did she seem the same as ever or at all troubled by something?"

"The last time..." Kiki tried to think about it. "She'd come into the spa every two-three weeks for her hair and a massage. Oh, wait, that's wrong. Inga and I saw her at Pinocchio's. It's a couple doors down from us. We went there on Friday night. We had a hard day—a bunch of bridesmaids and the bride showed up for facials and all before the wedding on Saturday. They were loud and giggly—really hard to take. But we knew Saturday would be worse—they're always busy. So we decided to 'de-stress.' Anyway, Audrey was there. She barely said hello to us and didn't introduce the fellow she was with. It was awkward, but it's not as if we're friends. We're hired help to her."

"The fellow who was with her—do you remember what he looked like?"

"Not really. He was nothing special. I guess I thought she'd be with somebody better looking. He might have been a client, come to think of it."

"Can you describe him at all?"

"He was sitting, but he seemed to be a big guy. Pudgy. I don't know if his hair was thin or what—it didn't show up much in the dark bar room lighting. He wasn't especially good-looking or noticeable. Although ..." She lightly touched her forehead. "I'm sorry. The old brain just doesn't want to work very well. But now that I think about it, I remember that when he saw me he looked startled, as if he was afraid I'd recognize him. Almost like someone caught cheating on his wife. But I'm not sure why."

"Well, if you remember anything more about his looks, or why he might have looked familiar to you, call me. You said he was big, with little hair ..." Rebecca paused. Why did that sound familiar to her? "Have you been able to remember anything more about the night you were attacked?"

"Only that he was another big guy. I'm not small, but he was tall and heavy-set."

"One more thing puzzles me. How did your attacker get into your flat to begin with? I know you have an alarm system, and a good lock on your door."

"Yes, but I disarmed the alarm since I was home."

"And the lock?"

Kiki looked puzzled. "He didn't break in?"

Rebecca shook her head. "There's no indication of that."

Kiki gave a sad and guilty look. "I always keep a spare key to my flat in the spa. I keep it there in case I lose my keys or something—so I can still get inside my house. I wonder if you look for the key, if it'll be gone."

Rebecca nodded. "Did anyone know about the extra key?"

"I don't think so, except for my kids, and probably my assistant, Inga. I think she might have seen me giving it to Esteban one time when he left his phone at my place and couldn't wait until I went home from work to go get it. You know how kids are with their phones."

Again, Rebecca nodded, as her mind raced with possibilities. If Inga and Esteban knew, others might as well. And if her landlord wanted her out of the spa, and somehow knew she had a spare key to her home in the spa, he could easily have let himself in after hours to get the house key. Perhaps Inga caught him there, and he killed her and then went after Kiki. It made sense ... but why kill Audrey who was needed to complete the deal? Should she be looking for two killers after all?

Rebecca soon realized there was nothing more that Kiki could add, and she decided it was time to leave. "Well, I'd better get going."

"One thing," Kiki said. "I'm wondering if I'll have a business when I leave here. Now that I'm not there to try to stop it, could you find out if my landlord is going to go ahead and sell? I know Audrey Poole was the realtor, but he could find someone else to handle the sale, I'm sure. And then where will I be?"

"I'll see what I can find out," Rebecca said.

"I spent a fortune on remodeling and permits for that spa. I don't want to see all that money going to waste."

Permits. It struck her where she'd previously heard the description of the man with Audrey. But there were plenty of heavy-set balding men in the city. Thousands, probably. But how many would know both Kiki and Audrey?

Rebecca sat back down. "I just thought of something," she said, and gave Richie a call.

In a matter of seconds, her phone vibrated. A photo had come through.

She handed the phone to Kiki. "That's the business card of a building inspector. Does his photo look familiar to you?"

Kiki studied it. "He's the man who inspected the building when we did our last remodel a few months back. We expanded the sauna area. And...yes, I'm sure of it. He's the man I saw with Audrey at Pinocchio's."

27

I s she still in the hospital?" Shay asked as he got into the passenger seat of Richie's Porsche. Richie was still waiting in the parking lot of SF General, growing more impatient with each passing minute.

"What the hell is she doing in there?" Richie wondered. He told Shay about her request to see the building inspector's picture but that he hadn't heard from her since. He stared out at the parking lot looking for her, his hands on the steering wheel and his fingers impatiently tapping it. "She trying to operate on her friend, or something? It should have been a quick in and out."

"She knows what she's doing," Shay's voice was calm.

"Like hell!"

Shay rolled his eyes.

"So, what are you doing here, anyway?" Richie asked, still fidgeting. "Other than criticizing me."

"I just wanted to see how you're doing," Shay said. "I know things aren't right between you and Mayfield. But it's also clear that you two care about each other. You want to talk about it?"

"Since when are you taking on the role of father confessor?"

Richie asked, tugging an earlobe. "Especially in matters of the heart."

"Maybe I'm just a good observer of human nature," Shay said with a bitter smile. "And I don't like to see my *paisan* in pain."

Richie's hands stilled as he studied his friend. "You've never spoken about any woman, but there is someone, isn't there?"

"No." Shay's response was too quick, and definitely too vehement. He then said, more calmly. "There isn't anyone."

"Was there ever?"

Shay shut his eyes a moment, then shook his head. Richie didn't know if he meant "No, never," or if it meant he simply refused to answer. Whatever it was, Richie knew Shay wasn't a person to press for an answer. To do so could mean alienating him forever. But when he was ready to talk, Richie would be there to listen.

"You're right about Rebecca and me," Richie admitted. "But I haven't figured out what to do about it. To be with her is complicated, and that makes it tough."

Shay nodded. Richie thought he wasn't going to comment, but he did, and his words were surprising. "There's always a cost, Richie. In your case, you both know it right up front."

"Always a cost. Leave it to you to cheer me up," Richie groused.

Shay smirked. "All I know is you're both unhappy. And I can't stand it anymore."

"So, I should get together with Rebecca so you won't be annoyed with us?"

"Exactly," Shay said.

Richie snorted. "I'll be sure to keep that in mind. But, since you're here," he added, "there's another thing I wanted to talk to you about. Audrey told me something that's been bothering me for days. It's just between you and me, okay? Don't say anything to Vito, to Rebecca, or anyone else."

Shay nodded his agreement.

"Audrey said her holding company is with Superior Savings in the Marina."

"Wait," Shay said. "Not the bank that Isabella—"

"Yeah, the same." Shay had been Richie's friend a long time. He had known Richie's fiancée, and he and Vito were the two guys that had pulled Richie out of the blackest, longest depression he had ever known after Isabella had been killed. "I'm sure there's nothing to it, but Audrey said the bank handled her offshore holding company because they made so much money on foreign transactions fees. And you know Isabella's job was as a loan officer. She had to look into accounts—the money that went into and out of them when anyone wanted to borrow or secure a loan, particularly when real estate was involved. It just gives me a bad feeling. I don't want to think anything weird was going on at that bank, but at the same time, I can't let Audrey's words go."

"You don't want to start seeing conspiracies and dirty-dealings under every mattress," Shay said.

"That's pretty funny coming from you," Richie told him.

"It makes sense for me. Anyway, you know how closely bank transactions are regulated," Shay said.

"I know a lot of stuff, but it doesn't mean I'm not surprised nearly every day by the shit people try, and often get away with. This thing has been niggling at me. I'm hoping, no, I'm praying that I'm wrong. But will you look into it?"

"Isabella's been gone four years," Shay said, his voice surprisingly gentle. "Are you sure you want to reopen all this up again?"

"Here comes Rebecca," Richie said, but quickly and quietly added, "I have no choice."

Shay nodded as he started out of the car. "It won't be easy and it won't be fast."

"Thanks. Go!"

Richie tried not to think about his conversation with Shay. Instead he studied the woman walking his way. Even with the black-haired wig and nurse's uniform, he'd know her anywhere. His admiration for her, for how she was handling all this, and wouldn't give up and wouldn't run, grew even more than he thought possible.

He hadn't yet figured out how to help her, but somehow, he had to.

"Was that Shay?" Rebecca asked as she got into Richie's car.

"He was updating me. Nothing new yet."

"Well, I may have a breakthrough. Let's go to Pinocchio's on Union. I want to talk to the bartender and cocktail waitress there again." Rebecca took off her wig and did her best to remove the dark eyebrow pencil as Richie drove.

Once at Pinocchio's, Rebecca showed the bartender the building inspector's business card. He said the man looked familiar, but he couldn't be sure why. The cocktail waitress's shift would start in a half-hour, so she was on her way to work.

Rebecca and Richie decided to wait for her. Richie ordered a bourbon and water for himself, a Mai Tai for Rebecca, and he carried them to the table where she sat.

They talked about Kiki's condition, the number of customers at Big Caesar's, and even Benedetta Rossi's house problems while they waited—anything but the subject that was on both their minds: their relationship.

Finally, mercifully to Rebecca's point of view, the cocktail waitress, Lisa Hayes, arrived. Rebecca handed her the building inspector's business card.

The waitress only needed a moment to study Darryl Kreshmer's photo. "That's him," she stated flatly. "Now that I see him, I remember him. I remember thinking, 'Surely, she can do better than that.'"

"So something made you think they were a couple," Rebecca said.

"Umm, I wouldn't go that far. I'm saying like, with you two, it's obvious—just the way you look at each other."

"But not with them?" Rebecca asked, trying not to think about how "obvious" a couple she and Richie were ... to an absolute stranger no less.

"With them, there was a weird undercurrent going on. Something about the way he looked at her made me think about it. I don't know. Maybe he was as confused about her being willing to meet him and buy him drinks as I was. I mean, the guy just didn't seem her type."

"But this is the man she was with?" Rebecca pointed at the building inspector's photo again.

"Unless he has an identical twin running around."

After the waitress left, Rebecca faced Richie. "It's time for me to talk to the building inspector."

Something about the way he looked at her, she was sure he was going to make some sort of crack about them looking like a couple. She scowled at him, hard.

"Okay, okay," he said with a grin. "About the building inspector, I always said Kreshmer was working with Audrey to find properties for her to sell. Remember how I found out that shortly after his visit to Benedetta Rossi, Audrey talked to her."

"God! Of course! It was staring right at me," Rebecca said. "Kiki told me Kreshmer showed up at the spa to check on a remodel. I suspect it wasn't long after that the owner decided to sell. Kreshmer was the stalking horse. The one that found properties Audrey might have been interested in. But that means he probably didn't kill her," Rebecca said. "After all, she was his source of income."

Richie nodded. "That would leave Sean Hinkle," Richie said. "He's the only one with the contacts and know-how to go after you for getting too close to figuring out what was going on."

"Great—a former date is now perfectly willing to have me killed. That doesn't do good things for a gal's ego, you know."

"It must have been a hell of a break-up."

"Funny." Rebecca grimaced. "But even though he might have the knowledge to send me to a fake crime scene, he would have no reason for killing Audrey. Just like Kreshmer, he would lose more than he'd gain by killing her, and there's no evidence he knew the other two women at all."

They both sipped their drinks.

"If everyone stood to gain from working with Audrey," Richie said, "and no one stood to lose, why are Audrey and Inga dead, and Kiki could have been as well?"

"We've got to be missing someone, or overlooking something," Rebecca said.

"Can your FBI friend help?" Richie asked.

Rebecca shook her head. "He would need something more than theories about a federal connection."

"I know you think he's not worthless," Richie sneered, "but I'd do whatever it took to help you if I had the power of the entire FBI at my fingertips. For cryin' out loud!"

"I don't want to ask him," she said firmly.

His jaw clenched a moment. "Okay, I've got some friends who might help. Let me talk to them."

Her eyes narrowed. "Is it legal?"

"You don't want to know. I'll drop you off at the Jade Dragon, and then I have to keep going. I've got to meet someone."

"That's fine, although I can't stay hidden there forever. One more night, and then tomorrow, I'm going back home and back to work."

He nodded. "Then we'll have to make sure we get the proof you need to put the killer away before that happens."

28

A fter Richie dropped Rebecca off at the Jade Dragon, he went to see Milton Jang of the Five Families Association to explain the crooked dealings going on. He had a plan that he hoped Jang would assist him with.

Richie wrote two identical notes and then had Jang's secretary type them up. She was asked to wear gloves as she placed them into envelopes. Jang would then have one of his runners, also wearing gloves, to deliver the notes directly to Darryl Kreshmer and Sean Hinkle.

The note read:

I have evidence that you killed Audrey Poole. Come to the alley behind the Jade Dragon with $50,000 in cash tomorrow at midnight, and I'll give you the evidence. If not, I'll turn the evidence over to the police.

Richie had no idea if either man would acknowledge such a note, but it wouldn't be the first time that greed and nervousness combined to make a killer do something foolish. He planned to wait there with some of Jang's bodyguards.

He didn't tell Rebecca about his plan. He wasn't *that* crazy.

29

Rebecca went back to Homicide the next morning. She would have to get her SUV back from Vito sometime soon. That morning, she took a taxi to work.

She knew she wasn't going to catch anybody by hiding in what was no more than an over-sized closet in Chinatown. She asked Sutter to join her as she went into Lt. Eastwood's office. There, she told both men about the phony call that led her to Baker's Beach two nights earlier.

"Once I got there, the man who called himself Officer Garcia was so strange, I knew it wasn't a legitimate crime scene, and I left." She didn't want to tell them about the shoot-out with the stranger or how she got away from him. Such a tale would lead to more questions than she wanted to answer.

"I think the person who sent me on the wild goose chase has something to do with city government," she said. "The only person involved in either murder with that background is Sean Hinkle."

"I was afraid you'd say that," Eastwood muttered.

"I'd like a search warrant for his home, phone, and computer," she said.

"You aren't going to get one," Eastwood replied. "He's too big, too important, and so far you have no evidence against him except a hunch."

"He called Poole the night she died, and his finances seem to be connected to hers. Plus, they were dating."

"Still not enough. I need hard evidence. He is, after all, on the mayor's staff."

"But that doesn't mean," Sutter said, catching Rebecca's eye, "that we can't lean on him."

Rebecca had an idea. She knew it was a long-shot, but sometimes they paid off. She phoned Sierra and asked Kiki's daughter to look up Sean Hinkle to see if he had ever been a customer at Kiki's spa. She knew Kiki didn't know him, but Kiki didn't personally know everyone who ever went there.

"He's here," Sierra said after a short while. "Let's see. He went twice for a massage. The last time was three months ago."

"Was Inga his masseuse?" Rebecca asked.

"Yes. Both times."

She thanked Sierra. She told Eastwood what she'd learned. "Enough evidence against Hinkle yet?"

"A lot of men get massages, Rebecca."

That evening, about an hour after most of the City Hall offices closed, Rebecca and Sutter went to Hinkle's apartment. It was time to "lean" as Sutter had said. Also, the last time Rebecca met with Hinkle, she had set up a meeting with him the next morning. She didn't make it because of the Baker's Beach incident, but apparently, he didn't show up for it either—almost as if he knew she wouldn't be there.

Almost as if he had arranged it so that he wouldn't have to answer difficult questions.

Hinkle lived in a condo high on Telegraph Hill, overlooking the piers of the Embarcadero, and the Bay beyond. He wasn't home when they arrived, so they sat in Sutter's car and waited for his return.

~

Earlier that day, Richie went to the Jade Dragon. Benny Wong told him Rebecca had left that morning for work. Richie guessed he shouldn't have been surprised. She'd been itching to return.

He called to make sure she was all right. She was. She told him she working with Sutter, and would try to catch up with him later.

He went in to Big Caesars for a while to take care of paperwork. As evening approached, and he still hadn't heard from Rebecca, he sent her a text asking her to meet him for dinner at the Jade Dragon at seven o'clock that evening.

He hoped that would keep her from going back to her apartment alone.

~

Rebecca saw Sean Hinkle's car turn onto the driveway for his condo's underground parking garage. As he waited for the gate to open, she and Sutter walked up to him. Sutter knocked on the window and showed his badge. "We need to talk."

Hinkle started, his eyes wide, as he looked from one to the other. He rolled down the window.

"We'll meet you inside," Sutter said.

Hinkle wet his lips, slowly regaining his composure. "Okay. My parking space is just past the entrance."

They followed while the gate was open. A few feet into the

garage, Hinkle parked and got out of his Prius. "What's this about?" he asked.

"Why don't we talk in your apartment?" Sutter suggested.

They rode the elevator in silence.

On the fourteenth floor, Hinkle led them to a small and sparsely furnished apartment. A balcony ran parallel to the living and dining areas, and the view from it made up for the apartment's lack of size and style.

Rebecca couldn't help but remember Hinkle's very old place on Valencia Street when she dated him. It had heating along the walls near the floor, and he had to kick the heater in the living room to get it to turn on. He'd come a long way in just a few years.

Hinkle didn't invite them to sit. Instead, hands on hips, he faced her and Sutter. "Now can you tell me why you've followed me up here? I'm guessing it's more than because I didn't bother to show up for the third-degree you wanted to give me, Rebecca. You knew I'd already told you everything I could."

"It's more than that," Rebecca said. "I want to know why Audrey Poole was afraid of you."

"Afraid of me? You're joking." Hinkle looked astonished. "You can't possibly think I had something to do with Audrey's death. Isn't it bad enough I get blackmail threats?"

"What blackmail threats?" Rebecca asked.

"Look." He handed her the hand-delivered note demanding he turn over money that night in Chinatown. Rebecca could scarcely believe what she was reading—especially the location "behind the alley at the Jade Dragon." Her mouth went dry, and she didn't want to consider who might have written such a thing.

"What are you going to do?" she asked, putting the note on the coffee table.

"Nothing. I'm ignoring it. I didn't do anything to Audrey! Why doesn't anyone believe me?"

"I've got an answer to that," Sutter said smugly.

Rebecca tried to put the note out of her mind. "Audrey went into hiding right before she died. She stayed in a hotel instead of her apartment, and she only had to finish a couple of deals before leaving the country. But something, or someone, convinced her to leave the hotel and return home."

"I know nothing about that."

"Except," Sutter said, "that you were one of the people who owed her money, a lot of money. Did you promise to pay her back? And then, after she met you, you killed her?"

"No!" Hinkle shook his head. "I owed her, but she wasn't afraid of me. I can't imagine Audrey hiding from anybody."

Rebecca took over. "But she claimed she was. If not you, who was she afraid of?"

"She once said she had some kind of crazy stalker after her."

"A stalker? You're saying a stalker killed her?"

"How should I know? All I know is it wasn't me."

"What did you talk about the night she died?"

"A meeting—"

"No. She had no charity meeting scheduled," Rebecca insisted. "She was trying to leave the country!"

Hinkle's shoulders sagged. "She was demanding I pay her what I owed." He shrugged. "I'd have loved to, except this city is so damned expensive, no matter how much I made, it was never enough. Besides, she hardly needed my pittance. She had plenty."

"We also connected you to Inga Westergaard," Sutter stated.

Hinkle stared at him a long moment. "Who?"

"The masseuse at Kiki's House of Beauty. You've gone to her; Audrey went to her, and now both women you know are dead."

Sean lifted his hands to his forehead. "You're joking, right? Why in God's name should I kill a masseuse?"

"You tell us," Sutter said.

"Look," Hinkle sat down on the sofa. "I don't know why you two think I'm involved in any of this, but I'm not."

"Not even involved in setting up a fake call from Dispatch that sent me out to Baker's Beach, alone, two nights ago?" Rebecca asked.

He opened his mouth as if to speak, then shut it tight.

She pressed. "I know you have connections with a lot of police in town. They could have easily filled you in on what's said and paying some young techie would have resulted in a clone of the dispatch phone number showing up on my phone."

Hinkle's hands curled into fists and pressed them to his knees. "It wasn't me, Rebecca."

"Who was it then?"

He shut his eyes and took a few deep breaths, then stood and walked over to the windows. There, he stared out at the lights of the city.

Richie finished his dinner, and Rebecca still hadn't shown up. He could see customers waiting for a table, so he told Benny to let his staff know that when Rebecca appeared, he would be waiting down in the room she was using.

He headed down there. He feared he would have a long wait. He couldn't help but remember the strange night they'd shared in that little room. He wished, more than anything, she were with him now, so he'd know she was safe.

He stepped into the room and from the corner of his eye noticed some movement.

And then he saw nothing at all.

30

Sean Hinkle stood before the picture windows of his apartment, staring at San Francisco Bay. Rebecca and Sutter were sitting on the sofa waiting for him to talk to them. As he turned and faced them, his eyes were troubled, even sad.

He crossed the room and poured himself some straight bourbon, asking if either detective wanted to join him. Both refused. After downing the glass, he faced Rebecca. "I've heard rumblings about you rocking the boat with some big investors, okay? I mean foreign types—not just Chinese, either. But especially some Saudis and Iranians. They've moved their money to Europe but are starting to get nervous over there. It's important for the city to be welcoming to them. To make it easy for them to buy good property here. Audrey was a key participant in all that. The last thing anybody wanted was for her to get killed. We were trying to present ourselves as a safe, diverse city. Then, our real estate agent got knifed to death on the street. How was that supposed to help anything?"

"Are you talking about politics?" Rebecca could scarcely follow what he was babbling about.

"No. Money. Big money. And things no one wants looked at."

It was beginning to make sense. As Richie kept telling her, it wasn't what she was specifically investigating, but where that investigation might lead, and who might be mentioned in the course of it, that was making "someone big" nervous.

"The mayor has his eye on the governorship," she said. "Maybe you're hoping he'll take you with him there. More money; more influence to peddle."

"Yes, I'm hoping the mayor will move up in the world. He deserves to, and I want to be there with him. But that's all the more reason for me not to go around killing anybody."

Sutter jumped in. "There's so much evidence—"

"No, there isn't," Hinkle interrupted. "If there were, we'd be having this conversation in your office, not my home. Rebecca's right, that I do have a lot of SFPD friends, and I know how these things work. I suggest you both leave now."

"We will be watching you, Hinkle," Sutter said, as the two detectives walked towards the door.

"I'm sorry it's come to this, Sean," Rebecca added.

"I didn't do anything to Audrey," he insisted.

"I know. It was her stalker." As she said it, she remembered Richie also mentioning that word. Could it be?

Sutter reached for the door to open it.

"Wait," she said, facing Sean again. "Did Audrey ever say who she was afraid of? Or give you more information about this so-called stalker of hers?"

"Rebecca," Sutter said quietly, shaking his head. She knew he didn't want her saying anything that might take some of the pressure off Hinkle. Switching to the possibility of a stalker could be interpreted as some kind of life line.

Hinkle shook his head. "She didn't really, but I know she was complaining about a guy involved in building permits. He'd give her a heads up on properties, but apparently he was telling her about places that weren't legitimate. It sounded like he was coming up with properties for her just for, hell, I don't know—either the money or to see her."

"A building inspector," Rebecca said. "Darryl Kreshmer, by any chance?"

"She never said his name. Just that she was going to have to break off contact with him."

~

Richie opened his eyes. He was on the floor, his hands duct taped behind his back, and his ears ringing from the blow his head received.

"Well, he wakes. One down, one to go."

He looked over his shoulder. Darryl Kreshmer sat on the bed, a revolver in his hand. "I wonder where she is."

Richie was filled with fury. This little nothing, well, a big nothing, was the one who had killed Audrey. Smart, clever, lovely Audrey. Somehow, he would make Kreshmer pay. "What the hell are you talking about?"

"Your girlfriend, the cop. She should be here by now. Where is she?"

"How should I know? Maybe she's not coming. Maybe she doesn't care," he muttered.

"That's not the way I hear it about the two of you," Kreshmer said with a snort. "She'll come."

Richie prayed Rebecca didn't come walking in on this madman. "Are you kidding me? You must have better luck with women than I me," he said. "I've been used and abused, let me tell you."

Kreshmer snorted. "A guy with your looks? I don't think so. I'm the one who gets treated like dirt."

"Looks don't matter," Richie said. "Audrey dumped me, too, you know."

Kreshmer's eyebrows lifted. "You went out with Audrey?"

"Years back. Many years. We dated a while, but then she ended it. She was just that way. Always had been. Did you know her long?"

Kreshmer shook his head. "I don't want to talk about her."

Richie saw that Kreshmer was close-mouthed, and so he spoke as casually as he could, given the circumstance, hoping to get the man to talk. "That's how I felt when she left me. Like my entire insides had been ripped out and thrown away. Did she care? Not at all. I think that's what hurt the most."

Kreshmer swallowed hard.

"It's too bad you didn't know what she was like," Richie said sympathetically. "If you did, you might have been prepared for the rotten way she treated you."

"I said, I don't want to talk about her."

"I know," Richie murmured. "Still, she had no business not appreciating all you did for her."

"How would you know?" Kreshmer spat out the words.

"I know that house on Francisco had no serious problems," Richie said. "But whatever Audrey wanted, Audrey got, right? And I suppose one of her 'buyers' wanted a house in that area, but didn't want to pay full price."

Kreshmer frowned.

"It's amazing how the rich get richer, isn't it?" Richie said. "They always get the best deals. It's the little guy, the middle income guys, who get screwed and end up paying full price for anything we try to do."

"It's the way the world runs," Kreshmer said. He marched over to Richie, his ham-like fist raised high. "Now, shut up!"

~

Rebecca and Sutter headed for Darryl Kreshmer's home. It was in an alley in the North Beach area, a small bungalow squeezed between a couple of larger houses. They contacted Lt. Eastwood, and he was working on getting a search warrant.

They parked in front of Kreshmer's house. Sutter's phone was in his hand when it chimed. "Let's go. Eastwood just texted. We have the okay to enter."

They knocked and rang the bell, but there was no answer. The building was old and wooden, and the door looked the same. Rebecca and Sutter nodded at each other and then struck the door at the same time with their shoulders. It sprang open.

They went in, guns drawn, but the place was empty. It was small—a living room, kitchen, one bedroom and one bathroom. And filthy.

They quickly searched.

"This may be it," Rebecca cried as she pulled a woman's handbag and jacket from the back of the bedroom closet. She put the jacket on the bed and opened the handbag. Inside the wallet was a driver's license. It belonged to Inga Westergaard.

"These are Inga's," Rebecca said. Kreshmer had to have taken them from Kiki's spa after killing Inga—that was the only way he could have gotten them. It was the proof they needed of his guilt. Rebecca could have shed tears of relief. "Finally, we've got him!"

"And look at this," Sutter said. He had opened Kreshmer's nightstand and found numerous photos of Audrey Poole. "It looks like we might have had a little obsession going on here. Many of these photos appear to have been taken from a distance —she's with other people on the street, in a restaurant, some taken through a window, as if Kreshmer was always outside, looking in and photographing the woman unknown to her."

"We've got to find him," Rebecca said.

"I'll start talking to neighbors and calling people shown in his computer," Sutter said.

Rebecca nodded. She had seen the text from Richie saying he was at the Jade Dragon, and she remembered the blackmail note Sean Hinkle had given her. She wondered how much Kreshmer might have known about all that.

She tried to call Richie, but got no answer. She texted him: *I'll be right there. Kreshmer is the killer. We have proof.*

She usually got a quick response from him, but now, nothing.

"I'm going to look for Richie," she said. "He knows Kreshmer. He might have some idea where he is."

"So Richie knows Kreshmer?" Sutter said with a sneer. "Why doesn't that surprise me?"

Richie's phone pinged. Kreshmer looked at it. "Oh, how sweet. She is coming. And she's warning you about me. 'Kreshmer is the killer,' she said. 'We have proof.' Well, this puts a new spin on things, doesn't it?"

"Go, Kreshmer. Just get out of here and run."

"And miss the fun?" Kreshmer said. "She's going to have to work a little harder to find you."

With that, he pulled Richie to his feet.

When Rebecca walked into the restaurant, the hostess immediately told her Richie was downstairs in "their" room—their love nest being the clear implication. Rebecca bristled, but said nothing as she headed to the back of the restaurant and down the stairs.

The room, however, was empty.

She went out to the alley and saw his Porsche. Where could he be?

She remembered the blackmail note Hinkle had showed her. It gave that very location as the drop for the money at midnight. Richie wouldn't, would he? She knew he would never be serious about blackmailing Hinkle, but he could have done it as a means to draw him out.

She called Shay who told her last he heard, Richie was going to wait to see her. And Shay knew nothing, or "claimed" to know nothing, about any midnight meeting behind the Jade Dragon.

Next, she phoned the assistant manager at Big Caesar's, Tommy Ginnetti, and asked if he had any idea where Richie might be. He told her the same thing—Richie had gone to the Jade Dragon to meet her.

She went upstairs and found Benny Wong in his office. She told him Richie wasn't in the room.

"I can't imagine Richie leaving his car, unless he walked over to see Milton Jang," Benny said.

"Jang?" Rebecca asked.

"Head of the Five Families Association. They were working together, and Jang used his runners to help Richie today."

Runners ... Hinkle told her the blackmail note was hand delivered. Her pulse began to pound. "Do you have a number for Jang?"

"Sure, but it would be best if you go to see him. He prefers to see who he is dealing with. He's just a block away. Ross Alley." He gave Rebecca the address.

Kreshmer marched Richie into the tunnel holding his revolver at his back and a flashlight in his other hand so they could see where they were going.

They went a long way before Kreshmer reached a spot where the tunnel forked, the main opening heading straight, and a smaller opening going off to the right.

Richie was told to turn right, and next thing he knew, Kreshmer knocked him to the ground. He fell hard, not being able to use his hands and arms to protect himself. Next thing he knew, a rope was being tightened around his ankles. Richie tried kicking, but all he got for his trouble was a hard smack in a knee with the butt of the gun. For a moment he feared the kneecap might have been broken, but eventually the sharp pain subsided.

Now, he sat up and leaned back against a wall. It was freezing down here in the tunnel, not to mention damp. There was water on the ground, and he had no idea if the water was from past rains that hadn't yet dried, or was from leaky sewage. The tunnel smelled bad enough it could have been the latter.

Richie could only think that if Rebecca did figure out where he was, if she heard him talking, she wouldn't walk into the trap Kreshmer had set.

"I didn't know you were a tunnel rat," he said.

"Shut the hell up," Kreshmer ordered.

"Why? We've got a lot of time and you know it. How do you know about these tunnels? Not many people do."

"Did you forget who I work for?" Kreshmer said. "I used to crawl under houses, through sewage systems, water mains, everything under ground, when I first started working for the City and County, before I worked my way up so I can order others to get covered with slime. I know more about the tunnels under Chinatown than probably anyone else alive today."

"Amazing." Richie did his best to go along with whatever Kreshmer said, to keep him calm and talking. But at the same time, he wondered why Kreshmer didn't just pop him—he'd already killed two women, and had tried to kill three. But as he thought about it, he realized Kreshmer must kill from raw emotion. It became Richie's purpose to keep the rage to a bare minimum. If he could.

~

Rebecca was stunned by the beautiful furnishings of Milton Jang's office. She realized as she waited, that he not only worked there, but he also lived in the building. She paced nervously as she watched the minutes tick by. Eventually, the door opened, and a small, older man entered the room.

"Inspector Mayfield," he said as he introduced himself. "I have heard much about you."

She didn't know how to respond to that—was it good or bad? She also didn't know if he was head of one of the "good" tongs, or the "bad" triads. Richie had told her a little about this world, but actually being here was so different from anything she'd ever dealt with, she found herself all but speechless.

"I'm here because I'm worried about Richie Amalfi," she said finally. "No one knows where he is, but his car is behind the Jade Dragon, and he was there before he disappeared. It might be that nothing is wrong, but he isn't answering my calls or texts. I was told you might be able to help."

Jang pursed his lips. "I've been waiting for his call as well. This isn't good."

"Why were you waiting?"

"He had an idea to send two similar messages. One went to Darryl Kreshmer, one to Sean Hinkle. We were going to wait and see who showed up. We expected one or the other would— to negotiate."

"I just came from Hinkle. He's not coming. But the building inspector might be."

"Kreshmer is a building inspector?" Jang asked.

"That's right."

"I see." He clasped his hands behind his back as he seemed to ponder all this. "The older buildings in the heart of China-town are very different from most in the city. Many are attached, almost all have alleyways in the back, and a good number of them lead to tunnels underground. A building inspector should know all that. And might know the tunnels as well."

Rebecca didn't want to think about the tunnels, but feared she had to. "The room I was given at the Jade Dragon is right next to an opening to a tunnel. If Kreshmer went after Richie, he could have used that to get to him, although the door did have a lock."

"And a building inspector can get through a locked door," Jang said.

"I've got to get down there," Rebecca said as she backed towards the door. "Thank you so much, Mr. Jang."

"Wait! You aren't going alone."

She stopped and faced him. "I'll be fine. I'll call for backup."

"And end up dead? The tunnels are narrow and have many areas where they split off. A man with a gun can lie in wait in one of those splits, and once you show up in a narrow section, you would have nowhere to run, no shelter to hide from the bullets."

That gave her pause, not only for her sake but also for Richie's. "What do you suggest?"

"I have several associates who know the tunnels well. Let me call them. They're Richie's best chance. And yours."

"But the time..."

"They'll be ready in ten minutes," Jang said. "I promise."

"What are you planning?" Richie asked.

Kreshmer chuckled. "That's a ballsy question."

Richie said nothing.

"If you must know, I'm going to kill you, and the cop you're in love with." Kreshmer chuckled to himself at that.

"I'm sorry this happened to you," Richie said softly, making his voice as soothing as he could. "I can tell you're no killer. It's Audrey's fault. She was a bitch."

"She wasn't!" Kreshmer insisted, aiming his flashlight at Richie's eyes, forcing him to turn his head away. "She could be nice. But she listened to the wrong people."

"Men, right?" Richie said.

"Men she worked with. They made her think she was going to get rich with these investors, but all that will change. The laws are being changed, and soon. I've been hearing about it. I tried to warn her."

"If only she'd have listened," Richie lamented.

"Foolish! So foolish!"

"You found good places for her to sell. You didn't need all those other investors. She would have done well enough with you alone."

"That's right."

"Just like the two buildings you found for her on Union Street," Richie said. "Two old, run-down buildings, side-by-side. One so much in need of work it was empty, an eyesore; and the one next to it, with an elderly Chinese couple upstairs, and a crummy spa on the main floor. The city would be much better off without those buildings, and Audrey would have made it happen—with your help."

"You know a lot, don't you?" Kreshmer sneered.

"I know a good deal when I see one. And that was a good deal, except for the spa's owner. She stood in the way, didn't she?"

Kreshmer didn't respond, but his jaw seemed to tighten.

"Without her, you would have been able to give Audrey everything she wanted, wouldn't you?"

"Audrey should have appreciated it."

"But, what I don't get was Inga. How did she stand in the way of anything?" Richie asked. "She was just a kid."

"She was no kid. She was a stupid, foul-mouthed adult!" Kreshmer's face reddened. "All I wanted to do was convince the owner to sell. I called and made an after-hours appointment for Audrey—she had bragged she was such a good customer they'd take her any time she wanted. I thought the owner would be there, but she wasn't. I tried to explain what I wanted to Inga, and to get her to tell me where Kiki lived. But instead of listening, she laughed at me. She said Kiki would never sell, and even if she did, it wouldn't get Audrey to care about me or to love me. She said even I should know that Audrey was just using me, and would dump me first chance she got. That little bitch wouldn't shut up. I warned her, time and again. Finally, I shoved that damned mud down her nasty throat. After that, I had no choice but to go after Kiki. I was searching for her address, and came across not only that, but her keys as well."

"I don't blame you," Richie said softly. "Talking to you like that, who did she think she was? And I'm sure she was lying about Audrey."

"No. She wasn't. That's why Audrey is dead, too. She told me it was over between us, that I was causing her too much trouble putting the screws on people like Benedetta Rossi. You ruined everything with your meddling!"

"Me? What are you talking about?"

"She said you went to her and complained about Benedetta's house. That she was sick of the complaints, sick of me always lurking around her. She said she was leaving the country. Leaving me! She tried to walk out on me so I killed her. And now, you and your woman are getting too close to me. I don't know how you did it. I was so careful. But, it doesn't matter anymore. Soon, you'll both be dead."

"You already tried to kill Rebecca once. But that didn't work out so well, did it?"

"What are you talking about?"

"The beach."

"What beach?"

Richie shut his mouth, momentarily surprised by Kreshmer's reaction. "It's nothing. Nothing, at all. No more deaths are needed. You can get away. Run. You've got time."

"You're wrong. Three more deaths are needed. Your nosy cop girlfriend, you, and then me." He looked up at the black mildew-covered ceiling, down at the wet ground, and then shook his head. "I can't go on after this."

"Listen to me--"

"It's over."

31

After ten minutes exactly, a woman entered the Five Families reception room. She kept her eyes lowered, her figure meek and subservient as she walked towards Milton Jang. She was dressed all in black, slacks, boots, a long-sleeved top, and a black scarf covering her hair.

She appeared to be in her forties or fifties, stood barely five feet tall, and was quite thin. Jang introduced her only as Little Squirrel. "She will lead you through the tunnels."

"But—" Rebecca thought he'd be amassing a minor army to help rescue Richie.

"You will be safe with her," Jang said.

"I'm sure, but Richie—"

"We will be sure he is safe, as long as he is not already dead." With that, Jang bowed his head, as did Little Squirrel.

Rebecca didn't like any of this. "Maybe I should call—"

"You will call no one. Follow Little Squirrel."

The woman, who had seemed meek and quiet up to that point, took hold of Rebecca's arm with strong, claw-like fingers. She started pulling Rebecca towards the door. Rebecca yanked her arm to free herself, but it didn't work. The woman stared at her, her eyes hard, and then let go.

Rebecca turned and faced Jang. "I'll go along with your plan because Richie considers you a friend. But if he was wrong to trust you, I won't let you forget it."

Jang said nothing and bowed his head.

Little Squirrel opened the door and waited for Rebecca to go through it.

In no time, they were back at the Jade Dragon, and down the stairs to the door that led to the tunnel.

Kreshmer heard a sound. He shut off his flashlight and turned towards the tunnel opening.

"*Don't come here, Reb—*" Richie shouted, but then Kreshmer spun around and smacked him in the face with the gun. Richie saw the swing coming and did his best to roll with it, but still ended up flat on the ground. He didn't move and his ears rang from the blow.

Kreshmer ripped a piece of duct tape from the roll in his pocket and slapped it over Richie's mouth, then turned his back on him and peered down the main artery of the tunnel in the direction of the Jade Dragon. Richie waited a moment for his head to clear, and using the wall as leverage, quietly tried to get back onto his feet.

Little Squirrel used a flashlight to light the way as she entered the tunnel. The last thing Rebecca wanted to do was to join her. It was bad enough knowing about the rats and spiders, the mold and the mildew, but she remembered Jang's words about the narrowness of the tunnel and it having few places to use as shelter.

"Be careful," Rebecca cautioned as she entered the tunnel behind Little Squirrel. She swallowed hard even as she reminded herself she had no choice. Richie was in there with a killer. "If he shoots at the flashlight, he could hit you."

They hurried along.

After about five minutes, Little Squirrel stopped, and shut off the light.

They were completely in the dark. With one hand on the tunnel wall as they went, the other on their firearms, they continued forward for several more minutes. Once the light was off, Rebecca could hear rats squeaking and running around, happy to be in the dark once more.

Several times, Rebecca thought she heard a muted thudding, as if someone might be kicking a wall, kicking the ground, or something. But in the dark, she could see nothing.

"Speak to him," Little Squirrel said. "He is near."

"How do you know?" Rebecca asked.

"I know."

"Kreshmer," Rebecca called.

No answer.

"Are you sure?" she asked.

Little Squirrel nodded.

"Kreshmer, I know you're here," Rebecca called. "Give yourself up."

All remained quiet, and then she heard a man's voice. "No. You're the one who has to give up if you want to see your boyfriend live. I'm sick of both of you, but you're the worst. You wouldn't leave well enough alone."

"You don't have to do this," she called.

"Don't waste your breath," he said. "I'm prepared for the consequences. You should be, too. You knew it would end this way."

Little Squirrel leaned close. "Say 'you win. I'm coming right now.'"

It went against all Rebecca's training to do that, but she did. "You win. I'm coming right now."

With that, Little Squirrel grabbed Rebecca and flung her backwards as if she weighed no more than a child, and then Little Squirrel ran forward in the tunnel. At the same time, lights went on all around them, portable spotlights so bright Rebecca was temporarily blinded by them. But she saw a large, balding man put his hands up to his eyes a moment before he stepped back, as if disappearing into a wall. She realized it was Kreshmer, and that he had found a spot where the tunnel forked and was hiding in one arm of it.

He fired a shot in her direction, and at the same time, Richie barreled into his back. Kreshmer was shoved away from his place of shelter out into the main tunnel opening while Richie dropped to the ground.

Shots rang out all around her.

Rebecca saw Little Squirrel on the ground and thought Kreshmer had hit her, but as quickly as it started, the gunfire stopped. Little Squirrel stood up and yelled something in a high-pitched angry-sounding Chinese. A man's voice answered, and then the lights went out just as Little Squirrel ran down the tunnel and disappeared.

Rebecca pulled out her own flashlight and moved cautiously until she saw the top of Kreshmer's head on the ground. From the way he lay, he was no longer a threat to her or anyone else.

She ran forward, rounding a corner, and there, on the ground was Richie, struggling to get loose.

She dropped to his side and ripped the tape from his mouth.

"Ow!" he cried.

She knelt beside him, seeing a gash on his cheek that was already starting to swell. "Are you all right?"

"Get this damned tape off my wrists."

She smiled with relief. "You're all right."

32

Sean Hinkle thought about the strange blackmail note he'd received. He knew why he received it, but any evidence shouldn't matter. He was no murderer. Other things, perhaps, but not a murderer. He hoped he'd managed to convince Rebecca and that Freddy Kruger-looking partner of hers of that.

He sat in his apartment. He loved living on Telegraph Hill with a view of the bay. He loved looking out at the new Bay Bridge, the water, the lights of the city all around him, and to know that it was his city. He planned to become mayor some day, not just a staffer. With money and connections he could do it. He could do anything.

The night seemed oddly silent. Usually the sound of cars, music, loud conversations, and even an occasional fog horn out on the bay could be heard. But not tonight. Tonight, he heard only the cool jazz he had coming through his sound system. He poured himself a glass of chardonnay and went out onto the balcony. Out there, he could hear the city sounds. He relished them.

He thought he heard a noise from inside his apartment and spun around. He saw nothing. No one.

It was probably the cat next door. An old gal kept one, and even though the condo had a no pets policy, he couldn't turn her in. He was, after all, a nice guy.

There was that sound again.

He was no scaredy-cat. Cat, ha! Hell, horror films were his favorite, so why was he letting a strange noise bother him? But the sound seemed to have moved closer and was now suspiciously like heavy breathing. A man's heavy breathing. That was no cat.

He spun around, but still saw nothing in his apartment. Was he hearing things?

Then, from a dark corner of the balcony, a form walked towards him.

"Who are you?"

His gaze dropped to the knife in the other man's hand.

It took a moment for it all to register. A fatal moment. The man walked towards him, and he backed up until he was against the banister around his balcony. Then, with one hand still holding the knife, the stranger sprang towards Hinkle, dropping the knife at the last second to put both hands on Hinkle's shoulders and shoving hard. Hinkle's leaned far out over the railing, but his hands still gripping it until his attacker bent forward and gave one last forceful push. Hinkle's hands, his rather delicate hands, didn't have the strength to hold the rail and to fight off the attack, not when gravity worked to pull him over the edge of the balcony.

His own scream as he fell fourteen stories was the last sound he heard.

33

That night, Rebecca learned an interesting lesson about Chinatown.

As she was helping Richie, to free him and make sure he hadn't been hurt, someone quietly carried Kreshmer's body out of the tunnel. As soon as she turned around to secure the crime scene and call for backup, she discovered she no longer had a crime scene.

"What the hell!"

"This way." Richie took her hand, and they ran out of the tunnel, back to the Jade Dragon, and then up the stairs and out to the alley.

There, she saw Kreshmer's body lying in the middle of the narrow alleyway, his gun by his hand.

She was all but beside herself with fury. "Who did this?" she demanded. "Who moved that body?"

A couple of uniformed officers who had been talking to witnesses, turned to see what she was saying.

"Stop," Richie said, pulling her away.

"Let go!" she demanded.

"Calm down and listen to what's going on around you." He

spoke through gritted teeth, trying to keep his voice low at the same time forcing her to pay attention to him.

"Is there a problem, ma'am?" One of the officers came up to her and Richie.

"I'm in Homicide," Rebecca told him. Seeing his worried, skeptical expression, added, "I'm getting my badge now—and I'm armed." She carefully removed the badge.

He looked it over.

"I was nearby," she said.

"Having dinner with me," Richie added. "When we heard the commotion. I couldn't keep her away."

She scowled at him, then turned back to the officer. "What's going on here?"

The officer explained that he and his partner were just a block away when a call came in to 9-1-1 about shots fired. When they arrived, they found the body in the alley. Witnesses told them the victim had stood in the alley waving a gun and making threats. A group of young men ran towards him and told him to go away, but he shot at them. They shot back, the man fell, and almost immediately died. The young men fled. No one saw which ones pulled the triggers, and it seems no one recognized any of the men who ran away.

Rebecca was stunned as she listened to all this nonsense. She also had to admit she was impressed that someone had the presence of mind to move the casings from Kreshmer's handgun into the alley for CSI to find.

As the uniforms went back to securing the scene and writing down witnesses names, Richie led Rebecca away from them. "There's nothing that connects you or me to Kreshmer's death," Richie said. "I suggest we leave it that way. In a sense, what the police were told was correct. A group of people from Chinatown did tell him to put down his gun, but he shot at them, and they shot back. No one knows who fired the fatal shot. What more do you want?"

"Milton Jang might know."

"He might. But if he says he doesn't?" Richie's gaze was hard. "Then what?"

Logic told her there was nothing she could do about it. She wasn't used to police work like this. It wasn't in the rules, not at all.

"Let it go, Rebecca," Richie urged. "Kreshmer confessed to Audrey and Inga's killings, and he wanted to kill Kiki. What more do you need?" He gave her a quick run-down of all Kreshmer had told him.

Rebecca was stunned. "So money, politics, and foreign intrigue had nothing to do with two people losing their lives," she said. "Amazing."

"It happens," Richie told her, and then said he was leaving.

"No! Kreshmer confessed to you. You've got to report what he told you."

"I don't like it. It opens up a can of worms."

Just then, the medical examiner and her team arrived. When Rebecca turned back to Richie, he was gone.

She felt overwhelmed, confused, and also angry. She looked around, trying to decide how much she should say in her report, and how much she should ignore.

Before making any decisions, she contacted Lt. Eastwood and told him Kreshmer was dead, and that she was at the crime scene. He sent Sutter to assist her in processing it, and said he wanted an explanation first thing in the morning.

"Rebecca, I've got a problem." Evelyn Ramirez called her over. "This body has been moved."

"Why do you say that?" Rebecca asked.

"There's not nearly enough blood here. No spatter from when the shots hit his torso."

"His jacket's pretty bulky," Rebecca said, wondering what was wrong with her. "Sometimes they absorb a lot more blood than we imagine they could." Not only did she lie, now she embellished that lie. She felt sick.

Ramirez frowned at the scene. "I've heard what was supposed to have happened here," she said. "I guess all those people telling what they witnessed can't be wrong."

"Who can say?" Rebecca asked.

"True enough. And this is Chinatown."

A few minutes later, Sutter arrived. "Isn't this the place I dropped you off earlier? And where Hinkle was asked to meet the blackmailer? It's strange that this guy freaked out right here, of all places, and got himself killed."

"Yes," Rebecca said, wondering how much more of this she could handle. "It is."

Then, from behind her, she heard Richie speak. "I called him to meet me here." She spun around, gaping at him. She thought he'd already left.

"I know Rebecca was trying to keep me out of this," he continued to Sutter. "But I was with her when the cocktail waitress at Pinocchio's ID'd Kreshmer as the last person seen with Audrey Poole. Audrey was a friend of mine, and I wanted the bastard who killed her caught. I'd talked to Kreshmer in the past. He knew I'm a ... shall we say 'fixer,' so when I told him I might be able to help get him out of these troubles, he came. We talked, and from what he said to me, I'm sure he killed Audrey and Inga. When I said he couldn't bribe Rebecca, he ran off. Later, Rebecca showed up to meet me. Kreshmer must have realized everything was closing in around him and went nuts and got killed for it. Who knows?"

Sutter frowned. "So I'm supposed to believe that for no good reason he confessed to you?"

"He thought I could influence Inspector Mayfield, which is

only more evidence that the jerk had no understanding of women whatsoever."

"We'll need your statement," Sutter said. "In writing."

Richie nodded. "You'll get it."

Sutter called over a CSI technician. "I want a gun powder residue test run on that man." He pointed at Richie.

Rebecca gawked at Sutter. "You can't think Richie—"

"Is there a problem with him taking the test?" Sutter asked.

"Not at all," Richie answered for her.

Sutter glared at him. "And I want to see you in Homicide tomorrow to complete your statement."

"You'll get it." Richie faced Rebecca before he went off with the CSI tech. "See you tomorrow."

She nodded. "Thank you," she said softly.

Rebecca and Sutter worked through the night. When they returned to Homicide, Lt. Eastwood was there waiting. He called her into his office to give him the low down on Richie's involvement as well as discuss the proofs they'd found in Kreshmer's apartment.

Eastwood seemed satisfied that Kreshmer was the killer—and Richie's gunpowder residue test was negative.

As they were finishing up, Eastwood received a call from Luis Calderon. During the night, he and Benson had been sent to a suspicious death on Telegraph Hill.

Sean Hinkle was dead, Calderon said. In his apartment, the detectives found a suicide note. It appeared he had thrown himself off his fourteenth floor balcony.

Rebecca was stunned by the news. She couldn't believe it, and neither could Sutter. Both suggested to Eastwood that

Calderon and Benson search hard for anything wrong with the "apparent suicide" scenario.

Before Eastwood allowed her to go back to her desk, he asked again why she and Richie happened to be in Chinatown last night. He was clearly digging.

"To have dinner, as I said."

He nodded. "It had nothing, I expect, to do with the note the CSI found in one of Kreshmer's pockets." He laid the blackmail note, covered in plastic, on his desk. "It tells Kreshmer to meet someone in that very location."

"Oh?" she said. "I haven't ever seen it before."

His gaze was hard and flat. "We'll look for fingerprints or anything else that might give us some idea who wrote it."

She blanched. "Of course. It's interesting that whoever wrote it knew Kreshmer was guilty."

"Maybe the author should be a detective instead of the staff I have."

She quickly left the office.

34

R ebecca had hoped to see Richie when he came into Homicide to give his written statement, but she was too tired to wait, and figured that if he was home sleeping, he wouldn't get there until late afternoon.

She did get a text from Vito that her SUV was in the Hall of Justice parking lot. She was grateful for that and used it when she left work. She had one stop to make before she went home and drove straight to the hospital to see Kiki.

Sierra and Esteban were both with her. They were thrilled to report that the doctor was sending Kiki home the next day. As long as she took it very easy for the next few weeks, she should be fine.

Rebecca's news of all that had happened with Darryl Kreshmer was equally well received. They were relieved to know that Kiki was no longer in any danger.

Kiki took a deep breath. "Love and death, they're always linked in some way."

"It's so sad that innocent people had to die," Rebecca said. "I'm only thankful you weren't one of them."

"So am I." She squeezed Rebecca's hand. "But I worry about

my business. Esteban says he'll be able to run things, and Sierra offered to help hire a new assistant, but I can't imagine anyone wanting the job after the horrible publicity Kiki's House of Beauty has received. I also can't imagine many customers coming back. The whole thing feels ghoulish. I know I'll think of Inga every time I walk into the place."

"Try not to worry. I'm sure Esteban and Sierra will do a good job for you."

"I know they will, but I can't help but think it might be time to let Mr. Young sell his building and move closer to his son."

Rebecca hated hearing Kiki say that, but it might be the most practical course for her and her children. "If you do decide to go that way, talk to Richie. He'll get you the best deal possible, believe me about that."

"You think he would?"

"I know he would."

Kiki sighed. "That's a relief."

"You don't have to decide right away. Let him talk to the buyers, see how much he can run up their offering price, and then see what works best for you."

"I like that idea," Kiki murmured.

"Get your health back, and after that, knowing you, Kiki, you'll be able to conquer the world."

Richie showed up at Rebecca's house that evening.

He greeted Spike, and then said, "I heard about Sean Hinkle's death. I just wanted to make sure you were okay after all this."

They faced each other awkwardly. "I'm okay."

"I've heard it was supposed to have been suicide."

"That's what Calderon and Benson's preliminary findings

are, but I understand they do have their doubts. His apartment was almost too clean, as was the railing where he jumped. But so far, they have no evidence at all to suggest it was anything else. And people at work are saying he's been despondent since his girlfriend, Audrey, was killed. They also hinted that he was involved in some of her real estate schemes. Even worse, the mayor was beginning to think he was a liability and was about to fire him, which they claim made him even more depressed."

"Do you believe it?"

"Not at all."

Richie nodded. "I wonder if he just knew too much."

"It could be. He was hiding something when I talked to him, but I don't know what." She sighed and moved towards her kitchen. "Coffee?"

He followed. "Thanks. I'm still tired from all that happened last night," he admitted.

"You gave your statement?" she asked.

He nodded. "Yes. I think Sutter will decide it's too much of a hassle to question any of this."

"I hope so," she admitted, handing him a cup.

"Kreshmer's reasons for killing had nothing to do with anything Hinkle was involved with." Richie took a sip of the warm brew. "But one thing troubles me. There's no suggestion at all that Kreshmer tried to have you killed on the beach. He was a loner, but he would have needed an accomplice at the beach. And I can't see him handling an assault rifle like a trained sniper out in that fog."

Her shoulder's sagged. "I know he told you he wasn't the shooter, but killing a cop is pretty much an automatic death sentence, and even confessing to an attempt might have been enough to take any plea deal off the table. And he did have enough connection in city government to find out how to fake the dispatch call to set me up. Besides, he had enough money, since he rarely spent any, to hire a hit-man."

"All that is true except for one thing. Once cornered, he didn't care about plea deals. He wanted to die. And another thing, I doubt if he had enough in his piggy bank to hire a two-man crew. Taking out a cop is a big deal. Very expensive."

"But if *he* wasn't the one who tried to kill me ..."

"I know," Richie whispered.

He said no more, but she could see in his eyes what he was thinking. Someone out there might have known what Sean Hinkle and Audrey were involved in and worried that her investigation might go a lot further up the chain of government or to some other powerful group—even the Five Families that Richie considered friends. If so, this wasn't over.

"As long as nothing new happens," Richie said, "no one should be coming after you again."

"I wonder if I'll ever know the entire story, and why Sean Hinkle died."

"It's safest not to ask." He finished his coffee. "I should go."

She followed him to the door. She couldn't help but lift her hand to lightly and gently touch his face. There was some swelling on the cheekbone, and he'd have a bruise for a while. It tore at her. "And I should let you," she whispered.

He looked all but pained at her touch, and at holding himself back. "I know, because you're Rebecca Rulebook."

"Maybe so." She dropped her hand as thoughts of all her lies about the "crime scene" in Chinatown and to her boss struck. "Or, maybe not."

As if reading her mind, he said, "Don't let it bother you. You did the right thing."

He looked down to see Spike up on his hind legs, his front paws on Richie's knees, begging to be petted. He reached down and picked him up. "Spike, my man, you take care of your Mom for me. She's a difficult one, but despite that, against any good sense I ever had, and all my mother's prayers to the contrary, I do love her, you know. And you." He kissed the top of Spike's head and gave the little guy a hug, then put him down. "Good-bye, Rebecca," he said softly, and then walked out the door.

She shut the door behind him.

She stood alone in the apartment. Spike gazed up at her with the saddest eyes she had ever seen, and she knew they were a reflection of her own.

—*I do love her, you know.*

She waited a moment, trying to breathe, thinking of all the times Richie had been there for her, and how does she thank him but to say she's "confused" and "troubled." Because of what? Because everything wasn't perfect between them? Because they had differences? Or was it because she had never felt so strongly about anyone and didn't know how to deal with emotions that seemed to defy her personal "rulebook"?

—*I do love her, you know.*

She couldn't stop herself from running out the door, through her back yard, and into the street.

She got there just in time to see his Porsche turn out of the alley. "Richie, wait!"

Too late. He didn't hear her, he didn't stop. Spike trotted outside and sat at her feet, looking up at her with a "What now?" expression.

"I don't know," she said, still looking at the empty street, scarcely believing he was gone. She could tell herself it was "for the best" that she hadn't gotten there on time, that her life would be much easier this way. But she didn't. "Spike, what have I done?"

35

R ichie sat alone at the bar at Big Caesar's. He tried talking to people; he tried playing the host, but his heart wasn't in it.

A number of people walked over to him from time to time to talk to him, but they soon realized—even if he said nothing unfriendly—that their company wasn't wanted that night.

And, he thought, why should it be? It was Saturday night, after all. The band was playing, the club was filled, but the only song that kept going through his head was "Saturday Night is the Loneliest Night of the Week" because that was how he felt.

Even Shay and Vito had kept out of his way the past couple of days, ever since the incident in Chinatown. He hadn't even felt like taking on any new clients. He'd had three guys come to him for help, but he turned them all away.

He had heard from Kiki, who was home now. He had gone to see her one day while Rebecca was at work. After serious thought and discussion with her children, Kiki realized that trying to get her spa going again after a dead body had been found in the mud bath, was probably a bridge too far. She was better off giving up the lease, resting until she was strong, and then finding a new location—with a new name—and starting over. She asked for his help.

Richie worked out a deal for her with Milton Jang, who did know a lot more about the potential buyers of the spa's location than he had been willing to admit when Richie first talked to him. The buyers wanted the property enough that they were willing to pay quite a bit to Kiki to void her lease. She was stunned and grateful. The money would go a long way to helping her set up her new spa when she ready.

Jang also found buyers for Steve Burlington's commercial building. Richie would net about five-hundred thousand dollars in that deal. He'd get a million from Burlington for closing the deal, but soon realized he would need to pay out at least half of that amount to everyone he worked with to make sure it happened.

He would do it this once, but never again.

Someday, he might even feel good about it.

He sipped his tonic and lime drink. He was quite tempted to have the bartender put gin in it, but he'd learned in the past that turning to alcohol to forget about Rebecca only made everything a lot worse.

He was surprised to hear the band start to play a song outside their usual swing and jazz numbers. He grimaced. "Unchained Melody." As soon as it began, he couldn't help but remember it was one of Rebecca's favorite songs, from one her favorite movies, the horribly sappy, romantic *Ghost*. Why, he wondered, was a woman who could be so sentimental over a romantic fantasy also be so hard-nosed when it came to real life and real emotions?

He turned around to get off the stool and tell the band he didn't pay them to play that kind of schlocky ...

Rebecca was walking his way.

He said nothing, only watched, as the center of all his

thoughts these past few days approached. She was wearing a black evening dress, her blond hair free of the pony tail she wore at work and hung soft and straight past her shoulders. She looked gorgeous. His insides felt as if they were doing hand-springs, but he also knew he couldn't jump to conclusions as to why she was here.

She probably came with that muscle-bound FBI creep and decided to say hello. He stiffened his shoulders. "Rebecca."

"They're playing my song," she said. Her voice was smooth as silk, a little low, with a bit of a catch in it.

"I know you like it," he murmured, and turned back to his drink, facing the bar.

She stepped closer. Standing beside him, she also faced the bar. She stared straight ahead as she murmured, "I was wrong."

He turned his head a bit in her direction. "Oh?"

"Nothing's changed," she admitted, catching his eyes. "Our issues are still the same as ever, but maybe we can find a way to deal with them."

He faced her square on, his expression bleak. "What's the good of that?"

"Maybe, in time, we'll figure it out," she said. "All I know is, I'd rather be miserable with you than without you."

His brows lifted. "So I make you miserable?"

"Absolutely," she admitted.

"Good."

"Good?"

"Because you do the same for me."

She smiled. "Dance with me, Richie. I did, after all, have to bribe the band leader to play my song."

"A bribe? Uh oh, Rebecca. Be careful of that slippery slope."

"Believe me, I am."

He got off the barstool and walked her to the dance floor. They only took a couple of steps when the song ended. He left her to whisper something in the band leader's ear. When he came back to her, he took her hand and said, "Now, it's my song."

The band began to play the jazz classic, "At Last."

And that was exactly what he was thinking as she stepped into his arms. He felt her softness and warmth; he drank in the heady scent of her perfume as their eyes met. Then her arm went to his shoulder as she moved closer. As they danced together once again, he knew that, despite everything that happened in the past and might happen in the future, at least for now she was back where she belonged. At last.

PLUS ...

Don't miss hearing about the next Rebecca and Richie story, and all of Joanne's new books by signing up for her mailing list at www.joannepence.com.

Find out what happens next in the lives of Rebecca and Richie when the clock strikes **SIX**.

Here are the opening pages of *Six O'Clock Silence:*

As I drive through quiet, fog-laden streets of the city, I'm filled with memories of all you once meant to me and how it all turned out so wrong.

I warned you. I taught you to fear. And ironically, it was me you came to fear. You couldn't see the real me. All you saw was your idea of me. All you heard were my words of warning, but not what was in my heart.

You were wrong. But I, too, was wrong to push you away. You and I never should have happened, but you sneaked up on me, wormed your way into my life, into my heart, with your goodness.

Yet, you weren't all that good, were you? If you were, you never would have cheated on the man you married. You didn't love him, that was clear. You loved him once, or so you claimed, but as the years passed, you grew into a dull acceptance of life, of boredom.

When we met, you said you had never known anyone like me. That I fascinated you with my silences, my strange life, and that I inflicted death on others with what you believed to be ease, and what I knew to be justice.

You said you loved me, but more than that, you feared me—feared me not for what I was, but for all I had come to mean to you.

I could not fight your fear.

In the end, I sent you back to the life you despised. And you hated me for it.

I vowed I would never contact you again, and made you promise me the same, even while knowing that together we were more than either of us is apart.

I ignored your tears as I walked away, and I didn't look back.

I have always been a man of my word.

Four days earlier—

San Francisco Homicide Inspector Rebecca Mayfield and her partner, Homicide Inspector Bill Sutter, stood at the edge of a trench dug to lay sewer lines in the far western portion of Golden Gate Park. The area, up to this time untouched by most park users, consisted of pine and fir trees, shrubs, a rarely visited old Dutch windmill, and a small tulip garden. But as the city's population grew, the Recreation and Park Commission decided to install public restrooms to prepare for future activity centers. The sewer lines would connect the restroom to the city system.

The trench was the length of two football fields, and deep. Along it were mounds of dirt that had been excavated.

As best Rebecca and Sutter could determine, none of the workmen had noticed anything unusual about the site until they arrived that morning. They found that something—most likely dogs or foxes—had dug through some of the dirt and scattered a number of small bones and one large one. The foreman believed the bones were human and called the police.

"I'd say the foreman is right," Rebecca said. Thirty-five years of age, she was tall, with large blue eyes in a triangular face ending in a pointed chin. Her straight blond hair was pulled back in a ponytail. "The bones look as if they're from a human hand, as in fingers. And the longer one could be a forearm."

The bones weren't the clean white color seen in museums or medical schools, but were a deep, mottled brown. All had been gnawed on, their ends ragged. But until someone with medical and forensic knowledge studied them, no one currently at the crime scene could officially state what they were looking at.

"I suspect," Sutter said, pointing at the undisturbed land on either side of the trench, "the rest of the body must be in there somewhere." Sutter was in his fifties, with short gray hair and a wiry build. He consistently spent more time planning for his retirement than thinking about his cases, but somehow couldn't bring himself to turn in the "I'm outta-here" paperwork.

"If someone buried an entire body out here," Rebecca said, "whoever did it picked one of the least busy areas of San Francisco. If those new sewer pipes weren't being installed, the site might have gone on undisturbed for quite a few more years."

"I always thought only vagrants and people wanting to hide from prying eyes come to this part of the park," Sutter said. "Seems like a waste of taxpayer money building restrooms way out here. No one, least of all me, ever expected this new construction."

Rebecca ignored most of the comment, but Sutter did have a point. "Which means, whoever buried the body—or parts of the body—here, must have assumed it would remain well hidden.

That it would never be discovered. It also means it's highly likely our corpse's death was no accident."

She walked away from the trench, Sutter following. "Let's get these bones packed up and to the lab, and shut this site down until we have a better idea of what's going on out here."

Continue with Six O'Clock Silence wherever fine books and ebooks are sold.

ABOUT THE AUTHOR

Joanne Pence was born and raised in northern California. She has been an award-winning, *USA Today* best-selling author of mysteries for many years, but she has also written historical fiction, contemporary romance, romantic suspense, a fantasy, and supernatural suspense. All of her books are now available as ebooks, and most are also in print. Joanne hopes you'll enjoy her books, which present a variety of times, places, and reading experiences, from mysterious to thrilling, emotional to lightly humorous, as well as powerful tales of times long past.

Visit her at www.joannepence.com and be sure to sign up for Joanne's mailing list to hear about new books.

The Rebecca Mayfield Mysteries

Rebecca is a by-the-book detective, who walks the straight and narrow in her work, and in her life. Richie, on the other hand, is not at all by-the-book. But opposites can and do attract, and there are few mystery two-somes quite as opposite as Rebecca and Richie.

ONE O'CLOCK HUSTLE – North American Book Award winner in Mystery
TWO O'CLOCK HEIST
THREE O'CLOCK SÉANCE
FOUR O'CLOCK SIZZLE
FIVE O'CLOCK TWIST
SIX O'CLOCK SILENCE

Plus a Christmas Novella: The Thirteenth Santa

The Angie & Friends Food & Spirits Mysteries

Angie Amalfi and Homicide Inspector Paavo Smith are soon to be married in this latest mystery series. Crime and calories plus a new "twist" in Angie's life in the form of a ghostly family inhabiting the house she and Paavo buy, create a mystery series with a "spirited" sense of fun and adventure.

COOKING SPIRITS

ADD A PINCH OF MURDER

COOK'S BIG DAY

MURDER BY DEVIL'S FOOD

Plus a Christmas mystery-fantasy: COOK'S CURIOUS CHRISTMAS

And a cookbook: COOK'S DESSERT COOKBOOK

The early "Angie Amalfi mystery series" began when Angie first met San Francisco Homicide Inspector Paavo Smith. Here are those mysteries in the order written:

SOMETHING'S COOKING

TOO MANY COOKS

COOKING UP TROUBLE

COOKING MOST DEADLY

COOK'S NIGHT OUT

COOKS OVERBOARD

A COOK IN TIME

TO CATCH A COOK

BELL, COOK, AND CANDLE

IF COOKS COULD KILL

TWO COOKS A-KILLING

COURTING DISASTER

RED HOT MURDER

THE DA VINCI COOK

Supernatural Suspense

Ancient Echoes

Top Idaho Fiction Book Award Winner

Over two hundred years ago, a covert expedition shadowing
Lewis and Clark disappeared in the wilderness of Central Idaho.
Now, seven anthropology students and their professor vanish in
the same area. The key to finding them lies in an ancient secret,
one that men throughout history have sought to unveil.

Michael Rempart is a brilliant archeologist with a colorful
and controversial career, but he is plagued by a sense of the
supernatural and a spiritual intuitiveness. Joining Michael are a
CIA consultant on paranormal phenomena, a washed-up local
sheriff, and a former scholar of Egyptology. All must overcome
their personal demons as they attempt to save the students and
learn the expedition's terrible secret....

Ancient Shadows

*One by one, a horror film director, a judge, and a newspaper
publisher meet brutal deaths. A link exists between them, and the
deaths have only begun ....*

Archeologist Michael Rempart finds himself pitted against
ancient demons and modern conspirators when a dying priest
gives him a powerful artifact—a pearl said to have granted
Genghis Khan the power, eight centuries ago, to lead his Mongol
warriors across the steppes to the gates of Vienna.

The artifact has set off centuries of war and destruction as it
conjures demons to play upon men's strongest ambitions and
cruelest desires. Michael realizes the so-called pearl is a philoso-
pher's stone, the prime agent of alchemy. As much as he would
like to ignore the artifact, when he sees horrific deaths and expe-

riences, first-hand, diabolical possession and affliction, he has no choice but to act, to follow a path along the Old Silk Road to a land that time forgot, and to somehow find a place that may no longer exist in the world as he knows it.

Historical, Contemporary & Fantasy Romance

Dance with a Gunfighter

Gabriella Devere wants vengeance. She grows up quickly when she witnesses the murder of her family by a gang of outlaws, and vows to make them pay for their crime. When the law won't help her, she takes matters into her own hands.

Jess McLowry left his war-torn Southern home to head West, where he hired out his gun. When he learns what happened to Gabriella's family, and what she plans, he knows a young woman like her will have no chance against the outlaws, and vows to save her the way he couldn't save his own family.

But the price of vengeance is high and Gabriella's willingness to sacrifice everything ultimately leads to the book's deadly and startling conclusion.

Willa Cather Literary Award finalist for Best Historical Novel.

The Dragon's Lady

Turn-of-the-century San Francisco comes to life in this romance of star-crossed lovers whose love is forbidden by both society and the laws of the time.

Ruth Greer, wealthy daughter of a shipping magnate, finds a young boy who has run away from his home in Chinatown—an area of gambling parlors, opium dens, and sing-song girls, as well as families trying to eke out a living. It is also home to the infamous and deadly "hatchet men" of Chinese lore.

There, Ruth meets Li Han-lin, a handsome, enigmatic leader of one such tong, and discovers he is neither as frightening cruel, or wanton as reputation would have her believe. As Ruth's fascination with the lawless area grows, she finds herself pulled deeper into its intrigue and dangers, particularly those surrounding Han-lin. But the two are from completely different worlds, and when both worlds are shattered by the Great Earthquake and Fire of 1906 that destroyed most of San Francisco, they face their ultimate test.

Seems Like Old Times

When Lee Reynolds, nationally known television news anchor, returns to the small town where she was born to sell her now-vacant childhood home, little does she expect to find that her first love has moved back to town. Nor does she expect that her feelings for him are still so strong.

Tony Santos had been a major league baseball player, but now finds his days of glory gone. He's gone back home to raise his young son as a single dad.

Both Tony and Lee have changed a lot. Yet, being with him, she finds that in her heart, it seems like old times...

The Ghost of Squire House

For decades, the home built by reclusive artist, Paul Squire, has stood empty on a windswept cliff overlooking the ocean. Those who attempted to live in the home soon fled in terror. Jennifer Barrett knows nothing of the history of the house she inherited. All she knows is she's glad for the chance to make a new life for herself.

It's Paul Squire's duty to rid his home of intruders, but something about this latest newcomer's vulnerable status ... and resemblance of someone from his past ... dulls his resolve. Jennifer would like to find a real flesh-and-blood man to liven her days and nights—someone to share her life with—but living in the artist's house, studying his paintings, she is surprised at how close she feels to him.

A compelling, prickly ghost with a tortured, guilt-ridden past, and a lonely heroine determined to start fresh, find themselves in a battle of wills and emotion in this ghostly fantasy of love, time, and chance.

Dangerous Journey

C.J. Perkins is trying to find her brother who went missing while on a Peace Corps assignment in Asia. All she knows is that the disappearance has something to do with a "White Dragon." Darius Kane, adventurer and bounty hunter, seems to be her only hope, and she practically shanghais him into helping her.

With a touch of the romantic adventure film Romancing the Stone, C.J. and Darius follow a trail that takes them through the narrow streets of Hong Kong, the backrooms of San Francisco's Chinatown, and the wild jungles of Borneo as they pursue both her brother and the White Dragon. The closer C.J. gets to them, the more danger she finds herself in—and it's not just danger of losing her life, but also of losing her heart.

Printed in the USA
CPSIA information can be obtained
at www.ICGtesting.com
LVHW091520201023
761671LV00005B/842

9 781949 566062